THE MISSING WHITE LADY

A PENELOPE BANKS MURDER MYSTERY

COLETTE CLARK

DESCRIPTION

Could a missing white cat be the key to solving this case?

New York, 1925

"My husband should be dead, but he isn't."

Penelope "Pen" Banks finally has what appears to be an interesting case for her fledgling investigative business. What she thought was a simple, tragic case of a wife abandonment has a rather daunting twist:

Jane Peterson's husband isn't where he's supposed to be—dead in Wilmington.

Pen soon discovers that Frank Peterson isn't the only missing resident from Winchester Court Apartments. Lady, the white-haired Persian cat of the Peterson's neighbor—an ever-partying flapper—has also disappeared.

There are strange goings on at Winchester Court, which

leads Penelope to believe the two are connected to something even bigger and more dangerous.

***Murder and the Missing White Lady* is the second book in the Penelope Banks Mystery series set in 1920s New York. The enjoyment of a cozy historical mystery combined with the excitement and daring of New York during Prohibition and the Jazz Age.**

ABOUT THE AUTHOR

Colette Clark lives in New York and has always enjoyed learning more about the history of her amazing city. She decided to combine that curiosity and love of learning with her addiction to reading and watching mysteries. Her first series, **Penelope Banks Murder Mysteries** is the result of those passions. When she's not writing she can be found doing Sudoku puzzles, drawing, eating tacos, visiting museums dedicated to unusual/weird/wacky things, and, of course, reading mysteries by other great authors.

Join my Newsletter to receive news about New Releases and Sales!
https://dashboard.mailerlite.com/forms/148684/72678356487767318/share

CHAPTER ONE

MANHATTAN 1925

"My husband should be dead but he isn't."

Penelope "Pen" Banks blinked twice in response. The woman sitting across from her was Jane Peterson, who had come this afternoon seeking her services.

Pen's lady investigator business was only just getting started. Still, she had managed to fully decorate the offices she'd leased on a whim. It was astounding what one could accomplish in a matter of weeks when one was swimming in kale. Her friend Benjamin "Benny" Davenport had introduced her to a "positively divine" decorator who had styled everything in some modern style called Art Deco. Pen rather liked the clean lines and geometric aesthetic done mostly in black and chrome against soft gold walls. She had never been one for clutter and knickknacks.

On the business side, Penelope would have been grateful to have a case worth taking on. Thus far it had been a rather dull affair. Her ad in the newspapers, offering affordable solutions to those who had not been taken seriously elsewhere, had produced a mere handful of cases.

Each of them had fallen into one of two categories: cheating husbands or missing pets.

Being that Penelope wasn't in this for the money—a very generous inheritance from an old family friend had seen to that—she was wondering if she had settled into the wrong game.

But this was certainly...different.

Jane Peterson certainly didn't seem like the murdering type. It was always the quiet ones, wasn't it?

Of course Penelope had only met one murderer in her life so she could hardly claim to be an expert.

Jane was a somewhat plain young woman with no makeup or jewelry beyond her wedding ring. She had yet to take the daring leap of cutting her light brown hair into a modern bob, as Pen's own dark hair was, and instead, it was pulled back into a loose chignon.

Still, there was a certain understated appeal in the way her pale blue eyes landed on Pen, like those of a lost kitten who needed shelter. Jane's hesitant smile instantly made one want to reassure her that all would be well. She was probably catnip to a certain kind of man who liked to play the knight in shining armor.

Perhaps this damsel had gotten fed up with being rescued?

"Mrs. Peterson, I'm not sure I understand."

Jane smiled faintly, but her eyes took on a sad note. "I know how that must sound but I thought it might be the only way you'd take me seriously. So far, everyone I've talked to is under the impression that Frank..." She paused, blushing slightly before she began speaking again. "Perhaps I should start at the beginning."

"Perhaps," Penelope said, still completely befuddled.

"My husband is a traveling salesman—he sells personalized Bibles." She smiled proudly. "He has a mobile device he uses to add gold lettering so people can put their family or Christian names on the cover. They're very popular and we're doing quite well in life."

Penelope eyed the woman's clothing. It was mid-February and still rather frigid outside so she'd had on a navy, full-length coat when she entered. It had been made of wool velour in a modern side-wrap style. Not extraordinarily chic, but definitely well-made.

The dress she was wearing underneath was brown and much more simple by comparison, the only decoration being scrolled embroidery also in brown. It was made of loosely draped silk that fell nearly down to the ankles. On her head, she wore a brown cloche hat with nothing more than a flat bow. It was all very fine quality with regard to material, cut, and design, but no one would mistake this woman for being either a flamboyant flapper or a wealthy socialite.

Frank Peterson was doing fairly well in life. Penelope wondered just how much these personalized Bibles sold for.

"Since he's paid on commission he's allowed to work as he pleases, which is nice since he only takes one week a month for his sales work. It's always the first week of the month because that's when a lot of people get paid and have enough saved up to buy their Bible. The rest of the month Frank and I get to spend together."

Penelope mulled that over and supposed that was a schedule that would work well for a happy marriage. Absence made the heart grow fonder, as they said.

"Last week was to be his week for sales. He was headed to Wilmington, North Carolina. At least..." Jane paused again, and a pleading look came to her eyes as she gazed at Penelope. "At least, he was *supposed* to be in Wilmington."

Jane reached into her small purse and pulled out a handkerchief. For someone whose husband was presumably alive when he should be dead, Penelope had trouble understanding why she was so distraught.

After dabbing her eyes, Jane replaced the handkerchief and pulled out a folded page from a newspaper instead. "I don't know if you read about the bus accident just outside of Wilmington?" Jane unfolded the newspaper and slid it across the desk.

It did sound familiar. Penelope had taken to reading the papers, mostly the crime and sensationalist material, all to see if she could use her skills to solve any recent mysteries.

The peculiar way Penelope's mind worked allowed her to instantly recall the article as though it was a photograph in front of her. Thus, she knew the incident to which Mrs. Peterson was referring. Still, Penelope scanned the headline in front of her, which was from a different paper: **Bus Goes Over Bridge, No Survivors**.

"As you can see, everyone on board died," Jane Peterson continued. "My husband should have been on that bus."

Rather than try to read the article, Penelope focused her bright blue eyes on Mrs. Peterson. "How did you come to learn he wasn't on the bus?"

"Well, I didn't at first, you see. When Frank is away, he often doesn't call me, though he promises to try and keep in touch. The places he goes and the people he sells to are simpler folk. He told me that in many of those towns, he wouldn't necessarily have access to a telephone. So, I didn't worry because I had no idea.

"I do make sure to have his entire schedule written

down, just in case. He left for Penn Station early that morning to catch the 8:45 train to Philadelphia, then onward to Richmond where he should have spent the night. The next day he was to continue on to Wilmington. At the tail end, he was to transfer to a bus. The bus that went over the bridge was the 7:05 from Jacksonville to Wilmington. That bus only runs twice a day, so he gave himself plenty of time to make sure he made it. Or at least, that's what he told me."

Once again, she reached into her purse to pull out her handkerchief before continuing.

"I don't normally read the papers, particularly when Frank is away. So much of it is so...." She shook her head as though she refused to even utter the appropriate word. "At any rate, I never would have known if I hadn't had lunch with my friend Betty. She happened to mention it because she knows my husband travels often. Betty tends to be rather insensitive about these sorts of things." Jane's mouth took on a bitter twist.

Penelope could understand. She'd had plenty of experience with so-called friends who liked to stir up controversy under the guise of concern. After abandoning her former wealthy and influential fiancé—who also happened to be a cheating scoundrel—she had been cut off by her wealthy father and left to fend for herself for three years before coming into a bequeathal of quite a vast sum.

"I rushed right out and bought a newspaper that day and...." Jane pointed to the paper still lying on the desk. "That's what I found."

She paused to dab her eyes again.

"Naturally, I called the offices of the bus company, but when I finally got connected they couldn't offer much information, at least at first. So, I traveled there myself and waited. They eventually released the names of all those on board at the time, those who had...well, you know. My husband's name was not on that list, Miss Banks."

"Perhaps the company made a mistake? Or maybe, your husband could have missed the bus and had to take the second one?"

"His time to be gone has passed, Miss Banks." Her voice was firmer now, and Penelope could sense the hint of frustration creeping in. "He was supposed to come back on Tuesday, as usual. That was *two days* ago."

She seemed ready to start crying again but caught herself.

"It's Thursday. He would have at least called or sent a telegram by now. I checked once more with the bus company *and* the local police for the names of the deceased, just to make sure. No Frank Peterson. If he wasn't among the passengers on that bus, then why hasn't he...?"

This was where she broke down fully. Penelope looked on in sympathy, allowing Mrs. Peterson a moment. Her mind worked as she waited.

A husband who, for all intents and purposes, simply disappeared once a week every month?

A husband who didn't usually communicate with his wife during that week?

A husband who now wasn't where he was supposed to be while he was away?

And now, a husband who had yet to return as scheduled?

It was definitely a case of wife abandonment. Still, this had a rather fascinating twist. What a horrible way of letting his wife know!

As though sensing Penelope's suspicions Jane quickly

recovered and met her with a direct look. "I know what you're thinking, the same thing everyone I've talked to thus far has all but stated, including the police. But my husband is no adulterer and he certainly hasn't left me. He loves me as much as I love him, perhaps more so. If you'd seen him when he was with me, you'd have no doubt. Only last month he'd been talking about starting a family. He was even more excited about it than I was. He'd take me on trips out of the city to look at nice homes with yards and fences, both of us imagining it." She paused, her eyes glazing over as though she were picturing it right then and there. They refocused and were once again trained on Penelope. "I came to you because in your ad you seemed to make a point of taking on cases that others have dismissed out of hand. My husband has not left me!"

"Of course not," Penelope soothed. Mrs. Peterson had a point; Penelope couldn't very well brush this off as a husband who'd gotten cold feet too late after his marital vows. She had to at least consider her potential client's protests. "Can you think of any reason why he wouldn't have returned or gotten in touch by now?"

Jane Peterson swallowed hard and her pale blue eyes grew watery as she shook her head. "That's why I've come to you Miss Banks, for an answer."

"Right," Penelope said. "How long have you been married?"

"It's been almost two years now. We would have started working on a family earlier but he wanted time for the two of us to enjoy marriage first. Frank likes to spoil me, take me out to Broadway shows, museums, shopping, even a simple walk through the park, just the two of us. He never thought he'd get married, you see. He always told me that until he met me, he assumed he'd live the rest of his life alone. I… thought the same would be true of myself."

The way Jane's cheeks colored this time made her seem almost pretty. She had a certain innocence that was no doubt easily impressed by Broadway shows and romantic walks in the park. She probably *hadn't* had many beaux prior to this Frank Peterson appearing in her life.

So why had he so suddenly disappeared from it?

"Were there any disagreements between you two? Anything he seemed upset about lately? Money problems? Work problems?"

"No, not at all," Jane said resolutely, her mouth tightened with resolve. "As I said, he is doing well financially and we hardly ever fight."

"I have to ask, of course. I don't charge very much and I only collect once the job is done, but I wouldn't want you to waste your money, all the same." When she'd first decided to take on this career, Penelope had wisely figured charging a nominal fee, and then only when the job was finished, would ward off any *completely* frivolous cases.

"Frank did *not* leave me, Miss Banks. I'll pay whatever you want to prove it."

Penelope nodded, accepting that she wasn't going to get an ounce of give on this topic.

"Do you have a photograph of your husband?"

"Yes, of course," Jane said, perking up now that Penelope seemed to be taking her case seriously. She dug into her purse again and pulled out a photograph. "He wasn't overly fond of having his picture taken. I don't know why, he's quite handsome as you can see. Still, I insisted we at least have one taken for our wedding, and he was happy about that."

Penelope accepted the photograph and studied it. Jane

played the part of the blushing bride quite well, even in black and white. It was obviously a small, simple wedding. The bride wore a modest, white day dress with a white cloche hat and held a bouquet of daffodils.

As for the groom, Frank Peterson did have a certain rugged handsomeness. He hadn't bothered offering a hint of a smile for the camera, but the earnestness in his expression was evident. In fact, there was a slightly menacing affect, as though anyone who dared question his devotion would be met with a bullet or a fist. He was facing away from the camera, slightly to his right. However, Penelope could see that there was a small patch on the right side of his face where the beard hadn't grown hair.

"Is that a scar on his face? Is that why he didn't like his photo taken?"

"Yes, but just so you know, he no longer has the beard. I think he realized that it made the scar more obvious. He's rather self-conscious about it."

He had no doubt wanted to present his best side for his wedding photo. Penelope thought that little flaw made him seem rather dashing in his own way.

Then again, Penelope had recently developed a certain fondness for men with scars. She suppressed an inappropriate smile, thinking about Detective Richard Prescott, whom she had met during her first bit of amateur sleuthing.

Perhaps Frank Peterson had also served in the Great War as her detective had? Though he seemed older than the average veteran of that conflict.

That addressed another revelation from the photograph, the age difference between the couple. Frank looked to be about twenty years older than Jane, who was probably around Penelope's age of twenty-four. Though from the look of him, the years had laid a harsher hand on him than most.

It made the contrast between the couple even more stark. He might as well have been Heathcliff from *Wuthering Heights* marrying Pollyanna.

Penelope's experience with men wasn't quite as *robust* as some, but she supposed that a man in his forties was less likely to be the sort to either marry or leave on a whim, especially with none of the usual grievances that motivate most men to desert their wives. The couple had yet to have children, and according to Jane, all was well financially. She also seemed like the compliant type, more likely to cater to his every demand than nag incessantly.

So where was Frank Peterson? More importantly, why had he not returned or even made some form of contact?

"You don't mind if I hold onto this photograph while I look into it some more, do you?" Penelope didn't need it, of course, but it might come in handy to present to people she talked with. Sadly, she already had the idea that it might be needed to identify an unclaimed body.

"Not at all," Jane replied almost breathless with relief.

"I'd like to follow up with you at your apartment or home. There might be some clues there that might help me learn more about what may have happened."

"Whatever you need to do," Mrs. Peterson replied without hesitation. Penelope considered that and decided Jane had nothing to hide as far as her household went. "I live in the Winchester Court Apartments. I'll write the address down for you."

Penelope smiled and handed her a pen and a sheet of paper.

Jane spoke as she wrote. "Thank you so much for taking this seriously, Miss Banks. I've been frustrated nearly to tears by everyone else who won't even consider the idea that Frank would never leave me."

When she finished writing, Jane lifted her head and met Penelope with that lost kitten look again. "I don't care what you find, even if he is in fact..." She choked up for a second but swallowed it. "Even if it's the worst. Just tell me what happened to my husband."

"I'll do everything in my power, Mrs. Peterson."

CHAPTER TWO

"Good evening, Chives," Penelope greeted when she returned to her 5th Avenue apartment that evening. It was the residence she had inherited from Agnes Sterling, almost five times the size of the one she had shared with her Cousin Cordelia in the three years prior. Chives had also offered to come along with the deal, which Penelope was eternally grateful for. She had left it to him to handle everything in this house, including her cousin.

"Good evening, Miss Banks," he greeted cordially. "Mrs. Davies has asked to see you when you returned. She's in the living room."

"Has she finally found a maid to meet her demanding requirements?" she asked, almost pleadingly.

"I believe so." Penelope swore she could hear the faintest trace of relief in his voice. It had been a grueling two weeks of interviews, during which Cousin Cordelia seemed to find fault with every candidate.

Penelope entered the living room, taking a moment to look out at Central Park through the windows. The apartment was high enough to see all the way to the Upper West

Side. Even in the rapidly approaching dusk, it was a lovely sight.

"Penelope!" Cousin Cordelia called out, an enthusiastic note in her voice.

She walked over to her cousin sitting on the sofa and sat down next to her. Across from them was a tall, slim woman about forty years old with a pleasant face, sitting perfectly erect in a chair. She had a sensible air to match her sensible attire and sensible hair in a low bun, which meant she no doubt had a sensible head on her shoulders.

"You've arrived just in time to meet Sally. I've offered her a position, I hope you don't mind?"

Penelope smiled at the woman. "If you're happy with her, then so am I."

"Nonsense, I'm sure you have questions? Concerns? Demands?"

"I'd like to think I'm fairly undemanding. I'll be gone most of the day," Penelope assured her. "Coffee in the morning would be lovely. Otherwise, your responsibility is mostly this one," she said tilting her head toward her cousin, who looked perfectly aghast at how casual Penelope was being about the whole affair.

"Really, Penelope. You're making us seem perfectly common."

"Well, we wouldn't want that."

"You'll have to forgive my younger cousin. You know how these bright young things are these days."

"Nothing but booze, jazz, and dancing," Penelope sang with a wave of the hand.

"*Penelope*!" Cousin Cordelia exclaimed, horrified.

Sally simply smiled. "Not to worry Mrs. Davies. I've worked in many a home with many different personalities. Not much startles or upsets me. My only concern is that the needs of those who employ me are met, hopefully to a degree higher than mere satisfaction."

"Well, I'm more than satisfied," Penelope said happily.

Cousin Cordelia sighed. "I suppose that settles it. So you agreed that you could come by as soon as tomorrow to get settled into your quarters?"

"Yes, ma'am."

"Perfect!" Penelope said, rising from the sofa. "I'm positively famished. I've had the most interesting day I want to tell you about over dinner, Cousin."

"Penelope is a private investigator," Cousin Cordelia said in a tone that was more apologetic than proud. She was still baffled at the idea that Penelope would want to have a job when she had only recently been left the sum of five million dollars.

"Oh, how fascinating," Sally replied, offering Penelope the look of appreciation her cousin had yet to grace her with.

"Yes, well, Chives will see you out," Cousin Cordelia said, rising to hurriedly see their new maid out before Penelope revealed too much, no doubt making them seem even more common.

When Sally was gone and Penelope had changed into more comfortable attire the two of them sat to dinner at a small table in the library rather than the grand dining room. It was much more intimate, and the floor-to-ceiling bookshelves offered a pleasant atmosphere.

"As I said, I finally have an interesting case," Penelope began as the first course was served.

"Oh, I do hope it isn't another poor dog or cat who's gone missing," Cousin Cordelia deplored, resting her soup spoon down.

"Nothing like that," Penelope reassured her, if only to

ward off her cousin's request for her "medicine," which was really nothing more than bootleg brandy that she once upon a time had a prescription for. Cousin Cordelia was nearly twice her age but had nerves that were more fragile than a newborn lamb's.

"A missing husband, but with an interesting twist." Penelope decided to fib about the details partially for privacy's sake and partially to protect her cousin's delicate constitution. "There was an accident in another city in which all the passengers were...injured. My client's husband was supposed to be on the bus involved, but he wasn't on the passenger list or in any of the hospitals."

Penelope had double-checked with the bus company herself, once she had finally been able to get through on the phone. It had certainly taken long enough, even for a long-distance call. No Frank Peterson.

"Oh well, thank goodness for that," Cousin Cordelia said pleasantly. "But then why ever did his wife need your services?"

"Because that's how she found out he was missing. He was scheduled to come back this Tuesday, and he still hasn't."

"Well, Penelope dear, I'm afraid it can only be one of two distinct possibilities."

"True," Penelope said, taking a sip of her contraband wine. "But there is still something odd about it. Why wasn't he where he told his wife he would be?"

"Again, I think we both know the answer to that, don't we?"

Penelope didn't really want to go into detail about the case. Mostly, it was nice to have someone to talk to about it, and perhaps offer a different perspective.

"If you had to think of the most outlandish explanation

what would it be?" she proposed, just to experiment with the idea.

"Oh Penelope, I have no idea," Cousin Cordelia said, getting flustered. She picked up her glass and drank a sip of wine, which was presumably an adequate substitute for her "medicine." After setting it down, she answered. "I do know that if he really loved her, he wouldn't put her through so much misery. My Harold would have walked through fire rather than see me so distraught. This husband of hers really doesn't deserve much consideration if he's simply disappeared on her. And to lie about where he was? Yes, Harold kept me from some of the more...*daunting* realities of life, but he never would have abandoned me."

Considering what Penelope knew of her cousin, Harold Davies would have had to keep quite a few things from his wife. Even Pen had to keep things from her. Cousin Cordelia still had no idea gambling at cards is what had kept them from being evicted in the three years before Penelope's gift from Agnes.

Tomorrow, she would visit Jane at the apartment she shared with Frank Peterson. Hopefully, that would provide more answers. After all, home was where the biggest secrets were kept.

CHAPTER THREE

The next day, Penelope arrived at Winchester Court apartments promptly at ten in the morning. It was a modestly sized, modern building located in the Upper West Side two blocks away from Central Park. The street was quiet and attractively residential, far enough away from the busiest streets and most of the attractions that drew people to New York City.

For such a nice neighborhood—this part of the city mostly housed the New Rich—it was a surprise to find there was no doorman. The building was five stories high. Counting the listings on the brass panel in front—no names, just apartment numbers—there were only twenty apartments.

Penelope pressed the button next to 2C, which Jane had indicated was her apartment. There was a speaking device next to it and she heard Jane's voice sound through.

"Miss Banks, is that you?"

"Yes," Penelope said through the device. She'd seen this tube system in other apartments so she raised her voice some.

Before Jane could come down to open the door for her, a tenant walked out and Penelope availed herself of the open door to enter on her own.

"Don't bother coming down, the door is open," she called out.

The entrance led to a small but elegant foyer with checkerboard marble flooring and a crystal chandelier above. There was a dual staircase that surrounded the elevator just ahead of her. The mailboxes to her right were brass plated just like the panel outside, all also labeled by apartment number rather than name.

Penelope disregarded the elevator in favor of the stairs, being that she only had to go up one floor. Before she even made it to the second-floor hallway she could hear the sound of boisterous voices drifting down toward her. At this hour of the morning, she would have expected the more subdued noise of people headed to an office job or wives headed out to do their daily shopping, but these individuals sounded as though they were leaving a party.

"Come, come, Daphne! Let's not dilly dally!"

The stairway emptied to the middle of the hallway. On either side of her were two doors, each across the hall from the other. It seemed 2A and 2B faced the street while 2C and 2D faced the back. Down a short hallway was a window that looked like it opened to the fire escape in back.

Although 2C was to Pen's left, the voices came from her right, which drew her curiosity. She turned to see people hovering near the open door of 2D. A man in a wrinkled dress shirt and slacks leaned against the wall, smoking a cigarette. His winter coat hung open to reveal bright purple suspenders, the top buttons of his shirt undone, and his red bowtie hanging loose around his neck. At one point he had probably looked very dapper, if somewhat foppish, but now his pomaded hair fell into his bleary eyes.

"Daphne my little flower, perhaps we've left too soon. It seems we have a *very* late party guest," he announced with a grin as he observed Penelope.

A woman hopped out of the apartment on one heeled foot. She was rolling a stocking up the other leg. She held her second shoe by the strap between her teeth. It was a red number with black sequins and a daring spiked heel. Her thick winter coat also hung open to reveal that her black lace and sequined dress was as disheveled as the man's clothes were. The kohl around her eyes had smeared enough to make her look like a raccoon. Her bobbed, brunette hair spilled in every direction around her head before she grabbed a hat to shove over it.

The woman pulled the shoe from her teeth and gave Penelope an apologetic smile. "Don't pay no attention to Spanky. He's still half-blotto."

Penelope flashed a brief, amused smile and headed the other way toward 2C. She knocked on the door.

"Hmm, it seems our daffodil has company, another *fleur* for my little garden, perhaps? What do you think, Daphne? I suppose I should stick with D, no? Daphne. Daisy. Daffodil. Now...a dahlia I think. She has that sort of proper look about her but with a bold flair. Yes, I think Dahlia is fitting."

Penelope turned to give him a wry smirk, then deliberately rolled her eyes back to 2C and knocked again. Where was Jane?

"You want to stop harassing my neighbors, Spanky?"

Penelope's attention was caught by the sound of this new voice, and she turned to see a young blonde woman make an appearance in the doorway to 2D...wearing nothing more than a thin chemise. She sipped something cloudy and white from a coupe glass as she joined the other two to study Penelope.

"It was a pajama party," she said with a wink in response to the way Penelope stared, perfectly agog. "These two are the last of the stragglers."

Penelope snapped her mouth shut. What kind of apartment building was this? It most definitely didn't fit with the image she'd had of the woman who came to see her yesterday.

The most recent member of the trio suddenly straightened up, her eyes widening. "Say, are you here about the break-ins? It's about time, I'll say."

"The break-ins?" Penelope asked, being that Jane seemed to be taking her time.

"The stuff people in this building had taken a few weeks ago. If the owners sent you, you make sure and tell them about my lady as well. I haven't seen her since my stuff was taken."

"She's missing?"

"Mmm-hmm," she replied, nodding and taking another sip.

Just how many people in this building had gone missing?

"Have you gone to the police?" Penelope asked.

The woman rested her hand on her hip. "What do you think the police are gonna do if I walk in saying my cat is missing? They'd laugh me right out of the station."

"Oh. A cat."

"Yes, *a cat*. And not just any cat, Lady was a purebred Persian, all white with long fur." She heaved a forlorn sigh. "My guy got her for me."

"I'm so sorry, but—"

"I mean, there's also the fur coat and the jewelry that was taken at the same time, but I can always get another fur or jewelry, ya know? How can I replace my precious Lady?"

"I'm not here at the behest of the owners," Penelope clarified.

"Behest?" Spanky repeated in an overly impressed voice. "I think we may have to upgrade this one up to a proper rose, darlings. What do you think, Daisy?"

"I think you two better get home and get that beauty sleep before tonight," said the woman in lingerie, presumably Daisy.

"Yes, yes, Daphne, let us be gone!" Spanky sang as he draped an arm around the other woman who finally had her second shoe on and buckled. They danced off, Spanky whistling some tune as they left.

Penelope turned to knock on 2C once again. "Daisy" remained in her doorway, leaning against the frame as she eyed Penelope and sipped her drink.

"So you're here to see that one, huh? She throwin' a party too? That would be somethin' new," she said with a laugh.

The door was opened by a perfectly mortified Jane. "Um, hello...um—"

"Jane, it's so good to see you again!" Penelope jubilantly greeted, broadcasting a broad smile as though they were old friends. She pulled Jane in for a hug, noting how rigid her body went in surprise. "It's been far too long."

"If you two need some champagne to celebrate this little reunion, I'd be happy to accommodate. Maybe I could finally learn something about my own neighbors," the other woman said with a wry smile.

"Thank you, no," Jane said, even though Pen was sure Daisy—if that was her real name—was teasing. Penelope wondered if Jane drank at all, even the "medicinal" sort that her dear Cousin Cordelia drank to calm her rattled nerves.

"Your husband out of town this week?" Daisy asked with a coy smile. "While the cat's away you two mice are playing, huh? Why *not* throw in some bubbly?"

"We're fine, thank you," Jane said in a weary tone, as though she was quite used to being taunted by her far more hedonistic neighbor.

"Thank you all the same," Penelope said in a pleasant voice as she entered the Petersons' apartment, thus allowing Jane to finally close the door.

She took a moment to quickly assess the inside. The decor made Penelope feel like she'd been transported back a hundred years to some Jane Austen novel rather than present-day New York City. Mrs. Peterson probably lost herself in romantic novels from that simpler time period. There was a lot of floral chintz to match the buttery yellow walls and heirloom furniture. No wonder Frank wanted to escape every month. Still, there was a certain quaint charm about it that appealed to the feminine sensibility. Even Penelope didn't *entirely* hate it.

It also further proved that there was money coming from somewhere. As suffocatingly precious as it was, at least for Penelope's own tastes, it wasn't cheap.

"Sorry about them," Jane said with an aggravated sigh. "She always has people coming and going, usually around the weekend. That's why Frank always comes back on Tuesdays. Like me, he'd rather avoid them."

"Well, one can't always help who their neighbors are."

Penelope had come planning to investigate Frank's past,

but something "Daisy" had mentioned sparked her interest. She figured she might as well address it first since they were on the topic.

"So," Penelope said, turning around to face Jane. "Tell me about these apartment burglaries."

CHAPTER FOUR

"The burglaries?" Jane repeated.

"Your neighbor—is it Daisy?"

"Daisy Fairchild," Jane said, grimacing slightly.

So that *was* her real name. "She mentioned that there had been break-ins in the building. Have you had anything stolen?"

"Nothing of any real importance. I mean, we don't have many valuables worth stealing. I had my checkbook taken, also some money. Frank has a box where he keeps important documents and old family photos. That was broken into. I suppose the burglar thought there might be something valuable inside, being that he keeps it locked in his closet."

That was interesting to note.

"Important papers?"

"Like birth certificates, our wedding license, things like that."

"And your husband keeps it locked?" Penelope wondered what other "important" things were in this box. Why would he keep it locked, especially since according to her neighbor, the Petersons didn't receive many visitors?

"I know he has things in there from his past. He doesn't like to dwell too much on that. He had a very unpleasant childhood. He's essentially cut himself off from his family. He hasn't been in touch with them at all since we've been married. I've never even met them."

How very convenient. Still, having been estranged from her own father for over three years now, Pen could understand not communicating with one's own family. At least Frank's had apparently left him with money, because Penelope was still quite skeptical that selling Bibles paid for all of this.

"So you've seen inside the box?"

"Of course I have," Jane said, her eyes flashing with umbrage. "Frank and I have no secrets from one another. I didn't even need to ask, he just showed me. There were photographs of his family, a few mementos, and official papers. That's all."

So he'd shown her, unprompted. Which would have given him a chance to rid the box of anything suspicious, thus satisfying any curiosity his wife might have harbored while keeping her from asking any questions.

"Was anything taken?"

"Just a small memento. A silver button."

"Anything else?"

"Not according to Frank. Why would he lie?"

Why indeed. It was now even more curious why her husband kept it locked. Most of the contents were harmless enough, silver button aside. What else had been in here that he didn't want his wife to see? Something that the burglar had taken, perhaps?

"When did this burglary happen?"

"Do you think it's related to Frank's disappearance?" Jane seemed uncertain.

"We investigators don't like to dismiss anything as irrelevant," Penelope said. She had no idea how real investigators operated but it seemed an unwise thing to do.

"It happened about three weeks ago."

So, only a week before Frank left for his usual vacation from his wife. Quite the coincidence.

"Do you know how many other people were burgled?"

"Frank and I mostly keep to ourselves." With neighbors like Daisy, Penelope could understand why. "Though, apparently the Middleberrys across the hall in 2A had some money and stock certificates taken. Some silver as well. She's the talkative type. Honestly, I don't see how this has anything to do with Frank."

"Anyone else? Perhaps on other floors?"

"Again, I have no idea." By now, Jane's impatience was growing.

Penelope decided it was time to move on. She removed her coat and led both of them over to a dainty little sofa to sit down. As she settled in, she realized it was an authentic Louis XVI era piece, reupholstered with Jane's beloved floral chintz to match the drapes. It must have cost quite a bit of kale.

On the table before them was a vase filled with silk flowers, daffodils like the ones in her wedding photos. There were small vases of them placed around the apartment.

"Does he buy you flowers?" Pen asked, mostly to put Jane at ease before she asked to look in that box of Frank's.

"No, not real ones. I always hated watching them wilt and die. These are much better don't you think? They'll last forever," she said, admiring the yellow flowers before them.

"That does make more sense."

"Then when spring comes, we go for walks and look at them all over the city."

Something in Jane's eyes faltered. Penelope could see she was detouring down the dark road that led right to Frank not being around to take her out to see the flowers this year.

"This box of his, can I have a look at it?" Pen dared ask if only to snap her out of it.

It worked. Jane's eyes went wide with alarm. "That's Frank's personal box. He wouldn't like me showing it to anyone."

"If Frank is in trouble, he would want you to do everything in your power to help him, Mrs. Peterson."

"Please...call me...Jane," she replied haltingly, still looking perfectly aghast at the idea of Penelope going through her husband's personal effects.

"Jane, this could be the one key that helps me find out where your husband is," Penelope said gently, hoping to coax her into compliance with what mattered most to her. "And I do have a strict rule regarding confidentiality. No one will ever know about what I find there, not even your husband, should he show up."

"Oh, Miss Banks," she fretted.

"Call me Penelope," she said with an encouraging smile. "This is probably more important than you know."

Jane finally relented and rose, escaping to the bedroom.

Penelope used the opportunity to explore a bit. She wandered over to the window and saw that this apartment did indeed face the back. There was a small garden behind the building, all the flora dead for winter. It was surrounded by a tall fence, high enough to keep trespassers out. A gate led to the alleyway that ran between the buildings.

Jane came back with a long flat box. The clasp at the

edge of it was still hanging by a small screw from when it had been broken into. She set it down on the coffee table in front of them. Penelope came back over and sat down, then gently opened the lid, cognizant of Jane's reluctance.

On top were official-looking papers, no doubt the important documents Jane had mentioned. Penelope flipped past the marriage license, a copy of the lease for the apartment, and other things that all looked to be perfectly unsuspicious. She found only two photographs underneath. Mostly out of curiosity, she picked them up to look at.

The first was of a young boy with fair hair and clear eyes staring ahead. He had just reached the age when parents began dressing boys in short pants. He was seated in a chair, holding a wooden horse in his hands.

"That's Frank's younger brother, Oliver. He died when he was very young," Jane said.

Penelope flipped it over. There had once been writing on the back, but someone had erased most of it. The only thing she could barely make out was: Oli...wit...fav...oy. No doubt it was meant to read: Oliver with favorite toy. Why would someone want to erase that?

Penelope noted that there were no photographs of Frank, even from his youth. Of course, men weren't quite as sentimental about these things.

She moved on to the next photo, which was of a man and woman staring at the camera with stern expressions. It was common enough for people to refrain from smiling in formal photographs, especially older ones, but there was something even more humorless and dour than usual about this couple. It lent credence to the idea that Frank hadn't had a happy childhood. Losing a child might create a somber and depressing environment.

On the back of this photograph were simply two names:

Marie and Thomas. There was no attempt to erase or otherwise hide this information. So why was it done to the other?

"So there were only two photographs?" Penelope confirmed.

"Yes, just his immediate family. He regrets not having one of his grandmother. She was who he was closest to. In fact, she's the reason for us meeting one another."

"Oh?" Penelope urged, turning her attention to Jane.

Jane's face instantly blossomed and Penelope could see what probably drew Frank to her in the first place if this was how she looked when she first met him.

"I was working at a wire service, to send money. Every month Frank would come in to send money back home to Detroit."

"I thought he was estranged from his family?"

"Oh no, not his grandmother, God rest her soul. She was the one bright light in his life, and he faithfully sent money to her every month."

"The first of the month?"

"Yes, that was back when he was working in an office of course."

So he sent money on the same schedule as his escape every month. Suddenly Penelope felt bad for Jane. Whatever this Frank was up to, Jane was too blinded by love to see it. Much like Penelope herself had been once upon a time, but at least she had seen through Clifford Stokes's lies before taking a walk down the aisle.

However, it was interesting that he was *sending* money home rather than receiving it.

"And how much was sent?"

"One hundred dollars every month."

Quite the generous grandson.

"He doted on her so," Jane said with a small laugh.

"The funny thing is, when she died, he found out she had been investing it all and left most of it to him in a savings account. That's how he was able to quit and... *forge his own path in life* with his idea about the Bibles. I just wish I could have met her. She died just before Frank proposed."

Another convenient coincidence. It seemed this Frank had a penchant for them. Penelope was almost certain the description for this brilliant money-making endeavor was Frank's. It would not have been difficult to convince Jane to approve of the idea with such empowering language.

"And he finally asked you out at some point?"

Jane laughed, looking prettier than ever. "It was the beginning of spring and the flowers had finally started blooming. I had always thought him this gruff, serious man. But one day, I honestly don't know what came over me, I commented on what a pretty day it was now that the first flowers were finally in bloom. The way he smiled at me, even now it makes me..." She paused, breathless and Penelope couldn't help but arch an eyebrow at the thought of what little Miss Jane was experiencing just then. "Anyway, he asked if I would like to go for a walk to see them after I ended my day."

By now her cheeks were perfectly rosy with pleasure. Penelope was sure it had all been very romantic. Even she couldn't find fault with his method of courtship. The flowers in New York *were* particularly lovely in spring.

"And this was...a little over two years ago?"

"Yes, Miss Banks."

"Penelope, please. I can see why he was so smitten."

Jane blinked in surprise, her cheeks now terribly red with self-consciousness. "Oh, Miss Banks..." she said, despite Penelope's insistence on using her first name.

"And your parents? They approved of the marriage?"

Penelope pressed before Jane became tongue-tied with embarrassment.

Jane's mouth tightened. "My mother and father...did not approve. They thought he was too old for me, even though they were always the ones to say that I would never even—" She swallowed and picked at her skirt. "My parents never complimented me, Miss Banks. When I told them I was leaving Poughkeepsie they did everything they could to prevent me from going, telling me I wasn't fit for anywhere else, that I could never make it on my own. There might have been something to that. I really only came because Betty, my best friend at the time encouraged me to come with her."

The same Betty who enjoyed revealing the news that Jane's husband may have been killed in a bus accident. Penelope had the idea this Betty wasn't much of a friend and had probably strong-armed poor Jane into moving to New York City with her.

"I was so terrified! I initially hated it here, even after finding a job so quickly. I thought my parents were right, that I'd be back in less than a year. Three months later, Frank began coming into the office I worked at. It's been like something out of a dream since then. I mean..." She looked around at her apartment with pride in her gaze. "Isn't it just wonderful?"

Penelope looked around and her eyes were immediately drawn to the mantle above the fireplace. Among the small little china figurines, there was a larger photograph in a frame of Frank and Jane on their wedding day. It was the only photograph on display in the entire apartment—Pen doubted Jane had any sentimentality about her own family—and appropriately seemed to hold a place of honor in the apartment.

"It's lovely. Frank has certainly spoiled you."

"He does—*did*." She blinked back tears. "He's dead isn't he Miss Banks?"

By now, Penelope was almost certain the man was in fact dead. If he wasn't, Jane might just wish he was if she learned the truth about him. Jane's parents obviously hadn't instilled anything resembling a healthy self-respect in their daughter. Penelope wasn't sure Frank had preyed on that or not.

Penelope rested a reassuring hand on top of hers. "Let's not make any assumptions just yet."

Jane sniffed back her tears and nodded. "So what do you think happened?"

"The morning he left, you didn't go with him to the station?"

"No, I didn't normally. He said that was part of *his* job, not mine. I simply made him breakfast as usual and kissed him outside in the hallway before he left." The tears finally came on the heels of that. "If I'd known that would be the last time I ever saw him—"

"We don't know that."

Pen turned her attention back to the box. "What is the memento you mentioned was missing?"

Jane collected herself enough to take a look inside. "It was a silver button from his grandfather's Union uniform during the Civil War. His grandmother gave it to him. Frank was incredibly upset about losing it."

That didn't seem suspicious. The thief probably thought it had monetary value. If it was from his beloved grandmother, it was no wonder Frank would be upset about it.

"Could it have something to do with why he's gone?"

"I'll look into it," Penelope assured her with a confident smile. "Why don't you tell me more about Frank?"

Jane offered to make coffee, which Penelope accepted. Anything to get Jane talking about Frank and her marriage.

By the time Pen had finished her first cup, she'd learned that Frank Peterson was the perfect husband. Almost too perfect.

It was obvious Frank had a history that he didn't want Jane to know about. And frankly, Jane didn't seem too curious about digging into it very much, perfectly happy to focus on her present and future with him.

"Well, I certainly have a much better idea of who your husband was. I can understand why you're worried. Trust me, Jane, I'll find out what happened to him. But...I do want you to be prepared for the worst."

"I can handle him being dead, Miss Banks. I'm already bracing myself for that."

"It might be something worse than that," Penelope risked revealing. "And I don't necessarily mean being unfaithful."

There was a brief flash of something steely in Jane's gaze before it was snuffed out and she returned to her fragile state. "I can handle *anything*, Miss Banks. Just find out what happened to him."

"I'll do my best."

Penelope got up to put her coat on and leave. Jane walked her to the door where they made their goodbyes. She got the feeling that Jane didn't want to risk encountering any of the other residents in the hallway. Thus, Penelope made quick work of leaving the apartment.

As soon as Jane closed her door, the door to 2A across the hall opened a crack and a woman peeked her head out. She stared at Pen with undisguised curiosity.

"I thought I heard a commotion earlier," she said, opening her door fully. She scanned Penelope's fine coat. "No, you're definitely not one of Daisy's."

Daisy's what, Penelope wasn't sure. But she *was* sure of who this woman was, Mrs. Middleberry, the resident gossip. She apparently had the ears of a hound, just waiting for Penelope to leave so she could sniff around to see what was going on.

Frankly, Penelope wasn't opposed to doing the same. Mrs. Middleberry would be a wealth of information.

"How do you do," Penelope greeted with a smile.

CHAPTER FIVE

Penelope had quietly corralled Mrs. Middleberry back into her apartment for coffee. It wasn't an easy thing to do, being that she was intent on chattering the entire way.

Pen certainly didn't want Jane to think she was gossiping with the neighbors. She had no interest in betraying Jane's confidence, of course, so she maintained the facade of being an old friend who had simply come by to visit.

Also, not a terribly easy thing to do, as it turned out.

"So you're one of Jane's friends?" Mrs. Middleberry asked, a dubious expression on her face as she poured coffee for Penelope. "I honestly didn't think she had any. I don't know if I've ever seen anyone come to visit in the nearly two years those two have lived here."

"Yes, it has been some time," Penelope said, shrugging in response to Mrs. Middleberry's skeptical look. "I kept meaning to visit Jane, but things happen."

"Hmm, I suppose." Mrs. Middleberry didn't look convinced.

She appeared to be in her early fifties and looked perfectly average with average brown hair pinned up at the back of her head, and an average house dress on, though it was nicer quality than most.

The apartment was an entirely different affair. If the Petersons' apartment looked like something from *Pride & Prejudice*, then the Middleberrys' looked like they had pinched every bit of furniture and decor straight from Versailles. Anything that could be gilded was, and the rest was covered in silk, damask, or velvet. One would think it would have turned out garish, but it somehow came together very well.

An aroma came from the kitchen that made Penelope's stomach ache with hunger. Being that it was almost noon, Mrs. Middleberry must have been making lunch when she caught Penelope.

"I think it's that husband of hers that keeps people away. Good looking enough, despite the scar of course, but he's definitely not a talker if you know what I mean."

"Jane seems happy enough with him." This conversation was taking a convenient turn.

"Well she's such a docile little thing, isn't she? She barely even speaks to me, despite how neighborly I am."

Penelope suspected she was more "nosy" than "neighborly" and perhaps that had something to do with it.

"And her husband Frank? Have you met him? I was hoping to meet him today as well, but Jane told me he's out of town for business." She had no interest in revealing that he was in fact missing, especially to the building gossip.

"Hmph, I'm not sure how much *business* gets done. He's always here! Except when he's gone of course. Gone longer than usual this time." She gave Penelope a knowing look that all but insinuated some very sordid assumptions.

At any rate, it confirmed that Mrs. Middleberry was a snoop of the worst kind, keeping track of the neighbors' comings and goings.

She continued on. "If you ask me, a man should have a proper job with a regular daily schedule. When my own Gordon first inherited all this money from his aunt, God rest her soul, he quit his job as a vice president at a Savings & Loan. Of course, *he'd* worked there for nearly twenty-five years without so much as a promotion, so we both thought he deserved a break. Anyway, it took a month before he was back to working again. Men shouldn't be idle. We had already given the house in Yonkers to our oldest and moved here to the city like I always dreamed of. Of course, it's a lot different from what I remember growing up—what with all the foreigners."

Penelope quietly sipped her coffee rather than express any agreement with that.

"Speaking of foreigners, I'm sure that Frank Peterson is one, though he hides it well, thank God. I happened to be passing in the hallway and overheard him speaking." Which most certainly meant she had her ear pressed to the door. "I think he was on the phone since I only heard his voice. But it *certainly* wasn't in English."

"Are you sure?" This was surprising news. Jane hadn't mentioned anything about him speaking another language. "What language was it?"

"Now, how would I know? I'm American, thank you very much."

"Did you happen to catch at least a few words or phrases?"

"It isn't as though I had my ear to the door or anything. I'm not a snoop you know. I just think it's a good idea to be familiar with one's neighbors. That's why we chose the apartment that faces the street, so I can see who comes in and out." Mrs. Middleberry smiled with satisfaction.

"So the Petersons don't get many visitors? I only ask out of concern for Jane, of course. I'd hate to think she gets lonely."

"No, which when you think about it is odd, isn't it? Even my family makes the effort to visit every once in a while, as much as they hate the city. But no, those Petersons haven't had a single visitor, not even that John fellow he keeps talking about."

"John?" Penelope perked up at the sound of a new name.

"John Keys—or maybe it was Key. I think Keyes makes more sense; I don't know, these doors are so thick it's hard to hear everything. Anyway, that husband of hers keeps telling her he's going to try to keep in touch with him. Obviously not someone he's ever bothered to ask over for dinner, since I've never seen him. Which is why it's such a surprise to see them finally have a visitor. Truth be told, like Daisy, I *also* thought you were here about the burglaries."

"You were burgled as well, I take it?"

Mrs. Middleberry reached up to fiddle with the string of pearls around her neck. Noting that it drew Penelope's eyes toward them, she laughed nervously. "I'm still shaken up over the whole thing. Thank goodness I keep these in a safe along with all my other jewelry. I knew the second we moved to Manhattan, I'd need to protect my belongings. So many unsavory types about these days. I kept telling Gordon to do the same with his things. After having our money, some silverware, and stock certificates stolen, you can bet he stores all his valuables in the safe now!"

"When did it happen?"

"Almost three weeks ago. I was out to do my usual

volunteering with the Daughters of the American Revolution—I go every Tuesday and Thursday morning. I didn't even realize we'd been robbed until I was looking for the silver bowl I use to serve nuts and it was gone! That's when Gordon and I looked around and found the other things missing as well."

"It must be someone who knows your schedule, or has at least seen you leave."

"You're thinking it was someone in the building too? I certainly have my eye on a few people."

"Really?"

"Well," she paused for just a moment. "I have to be honest, I did consider your friend's husband. Always here instead of working? And of course he would know if I was gone, living right across the hall. I've asked around and it's only been people on this floor who have been robbed...so far at least."

"You don't say," Penelope muttered, absorbing that information. That did make it very likely that it was a resident who lived on the second floor.

"This is exactly why I wanted a building with a doorman! Gordon put his foot down on that matter. Didn't want some stranger knowing when we came and went."

"So Frank Peterson is your number one suspect?" Penelope said, trying to get the conversation back toward her main interest.

"There are a few other suspicious characters I've had my eye on. For instance Adam Pulley just down the hallway in 2B. Now there's one who really keeps to himself. He's an author *supposedly*. But I looked him up at the library and didn't find any books under that name. Also, I always see him pacing the hallway or going up and down the stairs. I once asked him about it. He claims it helps him think.

What *I* think is, he's casing the place. That's what they call it, right, casing?"

It was plausible enough. He also had a ready-made excuse built in. Many people paced when they were thinking, and a change of scenery sometimes helped, especially if one was stuck in an apartment all day. Like the Middleberrys, his apartment had a window facing the street so he could see who came and went from the building. Had he taken a particular interest in Frank Peterson?

"Then, of course, there's that Daisy Fairchild, who is nothing but trouble," Mrs. Middleberry said with unfiltered disdain. "What a girl like that is doing in a building like this, I don't know. I was under the impression this was a respectable place with decent people. I certainly didn't expect to live next to some...*flapper*. She claims a fur coat and some jewelry of hers were stolen. I have a pretty good idea where *those* came from."

"Apparently her cat was taken at the same time?"

Mrs. Middleberry laughed. "Why would anyone want *that* creature? I mean, don't get me wrong, she's a pretty little thing. But what a nuisance! Always underfoot, wandering the hallways as though the entire building was hers. And leaving cat hair all over the place, mind you. I thought a house cat was supposed to remain in the *house*. I've even caught it sitting outside, though I had to tell that Daisy to stop leaving the window to the fire exit unlocked to let it out. She claims she doesn't, but I've seen that cat sitting out there just basking like the Queen of Sheba."

Perhaps Daisy's cat wasn't stolen so much as she had made a final escape. Wherever Lady was, it wasn't lazing outside in this weather. Penelope hoped she was someplace warm.

She thought back to when she'd been in the hallway. It

was carpeted, which would have certainly made it a target for cat hair. She hadn't seen a single strand, which meant the cat hadn't been wandering down it recently.

"Though, I can't blame the little thing. If I had to live in that den of iniquity, with parties and music going all hours of the night into morning, I'd want out too. Thank goodness these walls and doors are thick otherwise the manager of the building would be getting a piece of my mind!"

"Is there someone who comes to clean the hallways?"

"Of course, this isn't some tenement building, after all. Mr. Klukovich lives on the first floor with his wife. David and Ana, but I don't think those were their original names, if you know what I mean." She leaned in with one eye squinted. "*Eastern* European, but they seem safe enough. Not like the rest of them, you know."

Penelope kept her mouth shut, but certainly formed an even more unfavorable opinion of the woman.

"I know what you're thinking. I thought the same thing myself. It has to be those two, right? Well, the police apparently cleared them. Searched their apartment and everything. I still have my doubts, of course."

"Hmm," Penelope hummed noncommittally.

"They at least speak decent English," she continued, pulling back with a sigh. "He takes care of maintenance around the building. She keeps things nice and tidy. Though I could do without the grating sound of that electronic carpet sweeper every other day. Yes, I realize the daylight hours are ideal for such duties when most people are out and about, but we wives suffer for it."

The sound of a key turning in the lock of the front door drew Penelope's attention.

"Ah, speaking of wifely duties!" Mrs. Middleberry sang out. "That would be my Gordon, home for lunch."

The man who opened the door started in surprise when he saw Penelope sitting in the living room. He looked about as average as his wife, the sort of nondescript man one often saw shuffling along the sidewalk every morning and evening on his way to and from work. He eyed Penelope and his brow creased with worry. "Has something happened?"

Mrs. Middleberry laughed. "Oh no Gordon, this is Miss Banks, she was visiting Jane Peterson across the hall, I invited her over for coffee."

"But it seems I'm intruding on lunchtime." Penelope had only been granted half an hour for lunch when she'd held a job.

"Oh don't worry, now that he's a Vice President, he's allowed plenty of time to come home during the day. He's finally had his fill of lunches ordered at cafes and diners, haven't you dear? For the past month, he's been coming home to eat. There's nothing like my chicken pot pies, is there dear?"

Gordon smiled tightly as he shrugged out of his coat, still eyeing Penelope with uncertainty.

Mrs. Middleberry turned to Penelope with a proud smile. "He works at a special branch of the Savings & Loan down on...oh where was it, dear?"

"I'm sure she has no interest in that, Ida."

"East 35th Street, that's it! In between 5th and Madison, isn't that right?"

"Yes, but it's a very specialized branch, we only handle corporate accounts," he said with a forced smile, obviously in a hurry to get Penelope out of the apartment so he could eat. Heaven knew he had made quite the trek from 35th just to come home for lunch. Those pot pies must be delicious.

"I should be going. Again, I don't want to intrude. It was

nice to meet you both." Penelope rose up and neither party objected when she pulled her coat back on and left.

Once in the hallway, she waited for the Middleberrys' apartment door to close before she knocked softly on Jane's door. Hopefully, the distraction of her husband would keep Mrs. Middleberry from trying to listen too closely.

"Jane, I believe I left my pen here," she lied, just in case.

In response to Jane's quizzical expression, she subtly gestured to the door behind her across the hallway. Jane's eyes narrowed with understanding and she hurriedly urged Penelope inside.

"I just had a few follow-up questions," she said after Jane had closed the door. "Firstly, does your husband speak any other languages?"

"Frank?" Jane asked in surprise. She shook her head. "I mean, I've heard him say a word or phrase in Latin once or twice. He also learned a few French words, just simple sweet things to say to me. He always promised to take me to Paris one day, which I've dreamed of. Otherwise no, I don't think he speaks any other language than English."

"So, not enough to perhaps hold a phone conversation?"

Jane laughed uncertainly. "I think I would know if my own husband spoke another language. Why would he hide it from me?"

Why, indeed.

"I think that nosy Mrs. Middleberry probably just overheard him saying some term of endearment to me in French, which even he admitted he was terrible at, and she's making it into something it isn't."

That much could also be true.

"One more thing, do you or your husband know a John Keyes?" She said the name with deliberate pronunciation to see if it would spark something in Jane. "Or perhaps the last name was Key? It may be someone with whom your husband works? Mrs. Middleberry claimed she heard Frank mention the name."

"As far as I know he doesn't work with anyone, and no, I've never heard that name before." Jane looked more than irritated now.

"She may have misheard." Now Penelope was certain Jane was keeping something from her. Whatever it was had to do with this John Keyes—or Key fellow.

"Did she reveal anything more about me or my husband that I should know?" Jane asked in a somewhat testy voice.

"No, that's all," Penelope said, realizing Jane was in no mood to be forthcoming right now.

That didn't mean Penelope was done investigating. There was someone who might be able to provide more answers for her. Someone Penelope was quite looking forward to seeing.

CHAPTER SIX

Penelope stood in front of the building that housed the police department serving the 10A precinct of New York. It was more attractive than she would have thought for a police building, five stories tall with arched windows and stone columns built into the facade. Still, it fit in nicely with the Upper East Side aesthetic.

She walked in with a box in her hand and marched right up to the officer positioned behind the raised front desk.

"I'm here to see Detective Richard Prescott?"

"If you have a crime to report ma'am, I'm the one you talk to."

"Oh no, nothing of that sort," she said with a small, pleasant laugh. She lifted the box for him. "I've brought him his lunch."

The officer scanned her expensive fur-trimmed coat and matching hat with its fanned feathers, and his brow wrinkled in confusion. No, she looked nothing like a delivery girl, or presumably, a detective's overly doting wife.

"He really would prefer that I deliver it personally,"

Penelope urged with just the right amount of sugar in her voice, hoping that might prod him into accommodating her.

He shrugged and pointed the pen in his hand behind him toward the stairs. "Second floor."

"Thank you so much."

She felt a slight spring in her step as she took the stairs up. She wasn't sure if it was the prospect of clearing up a few mysteries for her case or the prospect of seeing the man who would help her do it.

The stairs led up to an open floor with multiple desks. She scanned them all, ignoring the curious looks from other officers and staff until her eyes landed on the face she was looking for. It wasn't difficult to miss, especially from her angle which provided an unobstructed view of the scar covering the lower half of his right jaw up to and including part of the ear, a memento from the Great War. It made his otherwise dashingly handsome face somehow even more attractive, at least to Penelope's point of view.

It had been a few weeks since she had last seen Detective Prescott, and even then they'd only known each other for a few days, though they had spent quite a bit of time together during those few days. Still, she felt a familiar absence of breath overtake her, all while the blood seemed to rush through her veins at a quickened pace.

She quickly overcame it, reminding herself that once he opened his mouth, the allure would be tarnished. He had a habit of irritating her as no other man could.

All the same, she planted a smile on her face and walked over to his desk. It took him a second to note her presence. When his eyes finally rolled up to meet hers, she could have sworn that, beneath the layer of understandable surprise, there was a note of pleasure at her presence. When facing him head-on, the scar was only barely noticeable, making him look like he should be on the silver screen instead of behind a desk.

He overcame his initial reaction as the cynicism set in. "Miss Banks, to what do I owe the pleasure?"

"I come bearing gifts," she said sweetly. "Or rather lunch."

Penelope had ordered the food from a quaint cafe on the corner near the Winchester Court apartments. It was then a quick taxi ride through Central Park to get here from there.

Detective Prescott's eyes narrowed with suspicion. "If I didn't know any better, I'd swear you were Greek."

She tittered dismissively and boldly took the seat next to his desk as she set the box down on top of it. "Don't be suspicious. It's only lunch, I promise. Ham sandwiches and potato salad, not an invading army hidden away in a wooden horse. There's even pie."

"This feels decidedly like a bribe."

"If you're going to be like that, I'll just have to give my rather valuable information to another detective to help him solve a case."

"I should have known there was an ulterior motive."

"No ulterior motive, just...a mutual boon."

The way he stared at her, in that damnably unreadable way, made her heated and self-conscious. She nervously smoothed the front wave of her bob into her hat as she lowered her eyes.

"Lucky for you, I have yet to have my lunch," he finally said, reaching out to slide the box closer to him and open it."What is it you would like in return, Miss Banks?"

"Haven't we moved beyond formal addresses?" she said, feeling flirtatious again. She raised her gaze to look at him and offered what she hoped was a pretty pout. "After all, we did solve two cases together, didn't we?"

"*I* seem to recall solving *a* case."

"With my help."

"And the other not being my case in the first place."

"But Glen Cove is surely indebted to you for it, no? I'll bet they owe you a favor."

"I'm not in the habit of holding favors over people's heads, *Miss Banks*. Speaking of favors...?"

"Ah, yes...I have a dead body."

He paused for a moment just staring at her, but she could sense the amused disbelief underneath the surface. "You do seem to collect those, don't you?"

"I do no such thing," Penelope retorted, highly offended. "It's the people around me who just happen to make them accumulate. Besides, this one isn't *necessarily* a body, at least on my end. It's a name."

"A name."

"Yes, that *may* be attached to a dead body."

"*May* be?

"Well, you see, he may not be dead."

"I see."

"Yet."

"That sounds ominous."

She could tell he was now taunting her, but she soldiered on.

"He also may not even be in New York."

"This is beginning to sound less and less like a boon for me."

"But if you have a dead body with no name it could be," she said hopefully.

Detective Prescott considered her. "Out of curiosity, what is the name?"

"Frank Peterson," Penelope said, perking up again. "Or perhaps John Keyes—or John Key."

"That's two names. Or three?"

"One may be the dead body, the other may be the perpetrator. Or perhaps a colleague or friend. But of course that doesn't necessarily dismiss him as the perpetrator."

"Hmm, a victim and a perpetrator. If only we had you on all of our cases in which a dead body shows up."

Penelope simply pursed her lips.

"I can hazard a guess that there are probably at least ten Frank Petersons in this area of Manhattan alone, never mind the rest of New York. John Key-or-Keyes is a little more unique, but again this is New York, there are probably still a hundred of them."

"But are any of them dead?" She briefly glared at him for the earlier insinuation. "It's for a case, nothing to do with me personally."

"That much I surmised. It seems the lady investigator business is off and running," he said as he opened the boxed lunch.

"Admittedly, this case has made it a more interesting endeavor."

Detective Prescott raised one eyebrow and a hint of a smile came to his face. Penelope was instantly reminded of their last conversation, in which the word "endeavor" had served as quite the euphemism. Against her will, she felt a flush rush to her cheeks.

Damn him!

Why did he always make her feel so naively innocent while at the same time scandalously provocative?

"Are you going to help me or not? Surely it's in the interest of the police force to put a name to a body, isn't it?"

"I can assure you that all our dead bodies in the 10A precinct are present and accounted for, Miss Banks."

"What about the other precincts?"

"Do you plan on going from precinct to precinct?" He gave her a mild look of surprise.

"No, that's your job," she said with a frown.

He laughed.

"What's so funny?"

"Presumably you did take note of the pile of paperwork on my desk as you approached...bearing gifts. I don't have the time to call every department to see if they have an anonymous body on their hands. A body that may not even exist, or even be in New York City."

"Don't you have a circular or bulletin or something that gets passed around different departments and cities that you can quickly scan?"

"That's a question for the newspapers. Which is where you *should* be hawking your gifted lunches, Miss Banks." He deliberately took a bite of the ham sandwich after saying this, which only raised her ire.

"I see how it is. It's only worth it if you can use me to your own beneficial ends," she said testily. "I suppose if you *did* have a dead body with no name you'd be thrilled with what I had to offer."

"I think any man would be thrilled with what you had to offer." The way his mouth cocked into a taunting half-smile made the double entendre glaringly obvious, but Penelope was in no mood to be flattered, embarrassed, or titillated.

"The women of Manhattan should be thankful services like mine exist. Heaven forbid they have to rely on the police force to do anything to help them."

"If you find your dead body, I'll be more than happy to

offer my services to help you find the culprit—*if* he happened to die in the area my precinct covers. Otherwise, I'll happily guide you to the right one, at which I am sure there are very competent detectives."

"And yet you were perfectly willing to go all the way to Long Island for another case."

"That was because I had nearly half a dozen of the wealthiest families insisting that I do."

"I can see this was a pointless endeav—mission," she quickly corrected.

Detective Prescott laughed easily and set the sandwich down. He leaned back in his chair to consider her. "Why don't you tell me what you have and I'll see if I can help eliminate a step or two for you? I suppose I owe you that much for such a savory gift, even without the accompanying horse."

Penelope held firm out of pure stubbornness before finally realizing the wisdom of using his experience. She told him all the details, pointedly making sure to include the fact that Jane Peterson had already gone to the police only to be told her husband had probably abandoned her.

"They were probably being kind. If he hasn't come back, and it's been several days since he was meant to, your Frank Peterson is most likely dead. Either that or he has no plans on coming back. I'm not sure which would be worse for her."

"The worst is not knowing either way."

Detective Prescott nodded in understanding.

Penelope pulled out the wedding picture to show him the couple.

He studied it. "So, we have a mid-to-late-forties male. Average build." He rolled his eyes up to her. "How tall would you say Mrs. Peterson is?"

"One or two inches shorter than me."

"That would make him about six feet...two, perhaps? Around my height. Does he still have the beard?"

"No, and his eyes are green, hair a shade of light brown." This much she had gotten over coffee with Jane.

"I see the scar on his face." If that struck any kind of note regarding his own scar, he didn't show it. That was one of the things Penelope appreciated about Detective Prescott, his complete lack of self-consciousness, as though his scar was no different than a man's choice to have a mustache or not. "How did he get it?"

"He told her it was an accident from a fall about ten years ago."

He handed the photograph back.

"If you need to hold onto it, you can. I'll remember what he looked like."

He smiled. "Ah yes, that memory of yours. I suppose it comes in handy for your profession."

"Yes, I remember *everything*." She gave him a level look, which made him grin.

"At any rate, I have a feeling the bride in this photograph would like it back. My memory may not be as impressive as yours but I'll remember and keep an eye out for him."

"Keep it, in case you do have a body you need to identify. She has another."

"If you insist. As I said, I will keep an eye out for any missing persons or bodies resembling him."

"I suppose I should thank you for that much."

"You said they had some things stolen?"

"A checkbook, some money, and a silver button."

"I suppose the silver button was worth something?"

"From his grandfather's uniform during the Civil War. He fought for the Union."

Detective Prescott frowned. "The Civil War? American uniforms didn't have silver buttons."

"Are you sure?"

"Not unless he customized it, which I suppose is a possibility. From my experience, the military isn't too keen on that, though it may have been more lax back then."

Penelope pondered that, then dismissed it as a low priority. "In the meantime, any other thoughts?"

Detective Prescott tapped one finger on his desk as he stared at the photo. "For some reason, it's the age difference that strikes me. It does happen of course."

"How old are you?" she blurted out before thinking.

He stared at her for a brief moment, that cryptic look on his face. "Twenty-nine at least for the next few months."

So about five years and change to her twenty-four years. That seemed young to be a detective, but what did Penelope know about the profession? Besides, so much about Detective Prescott seemed a surprise. How many detectives had graduated from Princeton, served in the war, and were well-versed in the world of art, three things she'd discovered about him when they'd first met?

"Happy birthday. *Preemptively*."

They both laughed.

"Why is the age difference so odd to you?"

"Not in and of itself. It's mostly that she has no history for him, other than his being from Detroit and estranged from his family. A man that old has at least *some* history behind him, even if it is a dull one."

"His may not be so dull."

"Exactly. Which makes it all the more likely that it's finally caught up with him."

"Perhaps," she said, mulling that over.

"Here's what I can do, I'll give you a card with the number to this station on it. If anything new comes up or you need my input, just call. Give your name when you call and ask for me."

"You'll answer for me?" she asked with a teasing smile.

"Only if I happen to need to put a name to a body," he said with a grin.

She pursed her lips as he wrote.

He slid it toward her. She reached for it, but he kept his hand on it, their fingertips nearly touching.

"Promise me you'll use this number before you do anything reckless. Again."

"I promise," she said, the picture of innocence.

Detective Prescott didn't seem entirely convinced.

CHAPTER SEVEN

Penelope returned to Winchester Court that evening after an early supper. It was still winter so the sun had already set by the time she arrived a little after six o'clock. The lights to several apartments were lit. From the opposite side of the street, she stared up through the windows, particularly those on the second floor. The Middleberrys had their curtains drawn, but Adam Pulley in 2B not only had his opened, but he stared out at the street as he smoked a pipe.

Penelope had the distinct impression he was staring right at her. Yes, she must have looked fairly conspicuous standing there in the freezing weather with her eyes focused on the apartment building, but there was still something rather unsettling about it. He didn't seem bothered by her watching, in fact, it seemed as though *he* was studying *her*.

Mrs. Middleberry had made him seem like something of a mystery. A writer who hadn't published any books, at least not under his own name? And all that walking through the hallways and stairs, supposedly in thought? Whatever he did for a living, it must have paid well to afford an apartment here.

From here, he looked to be in his late forties with light brown hair. The glasses he wore made him seem studious and the pipe gave him something of a professorial look. Hardly the villainous type, but perhaps that's what made it so easy for him to escape suspicion.

"Who are you Mr. Pulley?" she whispered to herself, a small cloud of white fog escaping her mouth.

As though he'd heard her, Adam removed his pipe and lifted it slightly, as though in acknowledgment of her presence. Penelope frowned, feeling even more self-conscious. No wonder Mrs. Middleberry was suspicious of him.

She shivered and hurriedly crossed the street to the building. Before she could press the button for Jane's apartment, the front door was opened and Daisy Fairchild walked out.

She was blessedly wearing a full set of clothes now. At least Penelope assumed she was underneath that fancy coat. This one wasn't a full fur, but it was certainly nice, dark wool with sable fur trim. She wore a cloche hat with beaded decoration.

"Well if it isn't our Dahlia," she greeted with a teasing smile.

"It's Penelope, Penelope Banks."

Daisy breathed out a laugh. "Nice to meet you, Penelope."

"Is your cat still missing?" Penelope asked, mostly to see if she could learn a little more about this string of burglaries. She also hated the idea of the poor creature perhaps being stuck outside somewhere. Mrs. Middleberry had indicated she was sometimes found on the fire escape.

Daisy's sudden change in expression plucked at Penelope's heartstrings.

"Yeah. I can't imagine why anyone would take her. I mean, I get the coat and jewelry, but my poor Lady?"

"Have you checked the building? I've heard she liked to wander the hallways."

Daisy narrowed her eyes. "I see that Mrs. Middleberry has been talking. Yes, I let her out sometimes. She likes to explore. She even found a little cat friend up in 3C she likes to go up and play with. They just moved in a few months ago. But Lady always comes back, *always*! It's been almost three weeks now. I can't help but think the worst. I just hope if the bastard did take her, he's treatin' her real nice."

"I'm so sorry."

Daisy offered a weak smile, then brightened up. "Hey, I'm having another party tonight, as usual. This one is gonna be in her honor. You should come."

"Okay," Penelope said slowly, then added in an uncertain voice, "What should I wear?"

Daisy laughed and lightly slapped her on the shoulder. "Don't worry, I was just teasin' about the pajama party thing this morning. You can wear whatever." She scanned Penelope's nice coat. "But I should warn you, it's a pretty *fun* crowd. Mostly folks from the Silver Palace."

At Penelope's blank look, Daisy laughed again. "Better yet, you should come see the show tonight. Catch me before I leave, it's one of my last performances there. I'm officially becoming a Ziegfeld girl! I got the news last month."

That was a name Penelope was more familiar with, but who wasn't? Everyone had heard of the *Ziegfeld Follies*, and many a young hopeful in New York clamored to be in the show. Pen had heard that it was extremely competitive, requiring a lot more than a pretty face, nice gams, and above-average talent.

"Congratulations," Penelope said impressed. However, she did wonder how a chorus girl could afford an apartment at Winchester Court. She wasn't too naïve or prudish to surmise where the money came from. Perhaps that same person had helped her get into the *Ziegfeld Follies*?

"Thanks," Daisy said, with a coy smile. It quickly disappeared. "I only wish Lady was here to celebrate with me."

Penelope thought about offering some comforting words, but if Daisy's cat had been gone this long, she probably wasn't coming back. Like Daisy, she also hoped that it was at least safe and cared for.

"The party is back here at my place after the last show, around one. You can bring the daffodil in 2C," she added with a giggle.

"Jane?"

"So that's her name, huh," At Penelope's surprised expression she smiled. "The two of them mostly keep to themselves. That husband of hers doesn't even look at me the way most men do. If he wasn't married, I'd have thought he was one of those...you know. Not that I have anything against that, I'm pretty sure Spanky is that way. He loves his flowers, doncha know," she laughed.

"He certainly seems to," Penelope said, unsure of what else to say to that. She knew a few people were "that way," one being her friend Benny Davenport.

"Anyway, I gotta grab this taxi," Daisy said, eyeing one driving down the street. She held the door to the building open long enough for Penelope to catch it then hurried on. "Don't forget to come to the show...or the party, either way. Bring a friend, the more the merrier!"

That would have meant a very late night for Penelope.

In the meantime, she wanted to press Jane a bit more for details about Frank. She probably should have waited until tomorrow, considering it was after normal business hours, but with a missing person, Penelope figured time was of the essence.

She hurried up the stairs and knocked on the door for 2C. When no one answered, she tried again, then pressed her ear to the door to listen for her.

Behind her, she heard 2A open.

"Are you looking for Jane?"

Penelope turned around, quickly thinking of an excuse as to why she'd be back to visit her "friend" so soon again. But her neighbor saved her the effort.

"She left a few hours after you this morning. Seemed to be in a hurry. Didn't even have time to say hello as she left," she sniffed.

"And she hasn't come back?"

"No, not at all." If anyone would be certain of that, it would be Mrs. Middleberry. She probably spent every hour that her husband was away at work sitting by her window watching her neighbors come and go. "Maybe she met up with that husband of hers?"

Penelope could hear the questioning tone in her voice and made sure her face gave away nothing. "I suppose I'll just have to catch her tomorrow," she said with a smile, escaping before Mrs. Middleberry got it into her head to start prying even more.

On the first floor, she decided to explore. Perhaps she'd find Lady hidden away somewhere, though it was unlikely. The stairway surrounded the elevators down to the foyer. Behind them was a darkened area that felt almost eerie. Pen imagined one could easily hide in the shadows here.

Penelope walked back out to the foyer to leave. While

she hadn't found the missing white Lady, she had perhaps found a hiding place for the burglar to take advantage of. She exited the building, hurrying along as she felt the eyes of both Mrs. Middleberry and Adam Pulley on her. When she was well out of range of their view, she slowed down to consider her options.

This party of Daisy's might be a good way to get more information. If she performed at night, it explained why her parties ended at around ten in the morning. It also meant she was home all day when these thefts supposedly took place. Maybe she had seen or heard something. Maybe the other regular party attendees had as well. It wouldn't hurt to go.

Besides, Penelope loved a good party, and this promised to be rather a fun one.

CHAPTER EIGHT

Before taking a nice long rest, Penelope had called up her friend Benny to invite him out much later that night. He was one who was always up for a bit of fun. He also had very few scruples so he'd be the perfect escort and private investigator partner. After all, he had played a small part in helping Pen discover who had killed Agnes Sterling.

Benny arrived at Penelope's apartment looking dapper as ever, with his hair perfectly combed back. His patrician features and expressive dark eyes made him handsome in a delicate sort of way.

Penelope was wearing one of the dresses she had recently splurged on now that she had kale to spend. It was a white silk, sleeveless number with a beaded v-neck. The skirt was made of lace, threaded with silver ribbon and even more beading, causing it to swish prettily with every step. Being that it was still winter, she had put on her white brushed wool coat with fur trim and scrolled beading. Her brown bob was adorned with a beaded head cap with white feathers sticking from the right side. Tonight would be her first real party since she'd inherited a fortune and she saw no reason to play it safe.

Leonard, the chauffeur she had *de facto* inherited from Agnes was now driving them to the Silver Palace. Benny had heard of the theater, *naturally*, and gave directions down to the Lower East Side.

"It's all the way on Houston Street?" Penelope commented in surprise.

That was certainly quite a distance from where Daisy lived on the Upper West Side. Penelope wondered why she didn't live in an apartment closer to where she worked. Though, it didn't matter anymore, being that she'd be much closer to her new theater. *Ziegfeld Follies* was right on Broadway.

Speaking of follies, Penelope wondered if this little detour from Jane's case was one. Even Pen had a hard time connecting Daisy's acting career with the disappearance of Frank Peterson. Still, she rationalized that it wasn't as though she'd otherwise be working on the case, so why not? At least this was tangentially related no matter how tenuously.

"The theater caters to a certain clientele," Benny said in an ambiguous tone.

Penelope studied him. "What do you know about it?"

"Nothing, Pen, I swear! I, for one, have never been. How could I possibly know what the performance is about?"

Something about the way he protested had her suspicious. Benny loved drama even more than Cousin Cordelia. But they were already almost there, just in time for the final showing of the night according to Benny's "sources."

Like much of New York City, this part of town didn't sleep. In fact, it seemed more alive this close to midnight than most other neighborhoods did in the middle of the day, especially on a Friday night. When one took a closer look at the establishments surrounding the theater, one could easily see why. Pool halls and smoke shops lined the streets. Those people spilling out of unmarked side doors strategically situated next to innocent-looking shops were completely zozzled; Penelope knew a speakeasy when she saw one. It was a wonder the police weren't permanently parked here. Perhaps someone had been greasing a few palms to look the other way.

"You don't have to wait for us, Leonard. We'll just get a taxi back," Penelope said when he parked near the Silver Palace.

"You sure?"

"I'm sure," Penelope said with a grin as she watched him eyeing three giggling young women in dresses that had taken quite a few liberties with the modern style of a higher hemline. Even in the February cold, they seemed determined to bare it all, wrapping their short coats around themselves as they flaunted their stockinged legs.

"If you insist, Miss Banks. I think I can find a way to enjoy the time off."

Penelope laughed. Leonard was in his early thirties and had the ability to charm a woman no matter how young or old she was. He'd even managed to get Cousin Cordelia, who once had a notorious dislike of motorized cars, to take advantage of his chauffeuring services on a regular basis.

"Just don't get into too much trouble," she teased.

"Yes ma'am," he said with an even broader grin as he got out to open the door for them.

Penelope felt energized by the throng of young, animated, tipsy people surrounding them. There was a wicked tinge in the air that made her feel daring. Benny looped his arm through hers and walked her to the theater.

They passed a nickelodeon and Penelope had to do a double-take at some of the black and white photos lining the windows.

"Zounds! Is that what I think it is?" she asked peering in closer.

"You'd know better than I would," Benny said in a droll voice, smirking as Penelope looked up from the photo of a woman wearing nothing but a strategically placed feather boa.

He tugged her away and led her to the Silver Palace where people, mostly men, were making their way in. Outside, the theater didn't look like much. At one point it had been done up to look like something grand and opulent, but the cracks of that facade were beginning to show. The grime of the city was sticking to the plaster and stone, and the painted parts hadn't been touched up in years it seemed.

The marquee outside read: **Garden of Delights**. The poster pasted near the front entrance showed an illustration of rosy-cheeked women dressed as flowers, but with plenty of bare arms and legs on display. Underneath she saw Daisy Fairchild and Daphne Lavoie listed among the performers among others. A Spencer Ankara had produced and written the show. Penelope wondered if that was "Spanky."

"I guess I know what kind of show this is then," she wryly remarked.

Benny chuckled next to her as he led the way in. "I've always been curious about burlesque. Supposedly there's an art to it, and it's supposed to be a slapper. At least we should get a few laughs."

"Yes, I'm sure that's the appeal," Penelope replied in a sardonic voice.

They entered and bought their tickets. The interior of the Silver Palace was slightly more aesthetically appealing than the outside, at least from what little Penelope could see in the dim lighting. No doubt that effect was to help set the sordid tone to what the audience would soon be exposed to.

It was all rather thrilling. Penelope had done some risqué things during her tenure playing cards to earn money. Most of that had fallen in the category of drinking and gambling. Sins of the flesh were an entirely different world. She was glad she'd asked Benny to accompany her, even if he was the sort that was unlikely to play the strong, masculine hero.

"Once again Pen, I have to congratulate you on being the most interesting person I know. Tell me again how this is related to your case?" Benny asked as they took their seats and waited for the show to begin.

"I'm not sure that it is. Mostly I'm interested in the party afterward back at her apartment. There's been a string of burglaries in the building. They seem to have happened during the day when Daisy is presumably home asleep. All on the second floor, as far as I know. So I think it's someone who lives on that floor or someone who visits regularly. Say, for instance, someone who regularly attends a party thrown by the resident flapper? At the very least, maybe someone has seen something when they leave the parties in the early morning."

"Be honest, you just want to go to a party, don't you?"

"Always, darling," Penelope said with a laugh, quieting down as the lights lowered and the music started.

The curtains rose to a lush, picturesque scene reminiscent of a wild garden. Gradually, the oversized flowers on stage "blossomed" to reveal themselves as scantily clad women, each wearing colorful matching wigs. That was perhaps the only innocent part of the entire night's performance. By the end of it, Penelope could understand why Daisy had felt no shame being seen in nothing but a chemise that morning.

What was glaringly apparent was that Daisy Fairchild was the undisputed star of the show. She did have talent, a lovely singing voice, and a certain gracefulness to her movements, which were mostly unburdened by too much clothing. She was also strikingly beautiful when her hair and makeup were done up for the stage.

It was a wonder how—or why?—Frank Peterson had shown absolutely no interest in her.

By the end, Penelope had a good idea of what Eve must have felt after tasting the forbidden fruit. But in her mind, there was no such thing as too much knowledge, no matter how lascivious. After all, who knew what future cases might hold for her?

"Well, that was—are we sure that was burlesque? I thought it was supposed to be more like a minstrel show, maybe with a bit of low humor and women in petticoats and things?" she asked as Benny and she left the theater.

Benny laughed. "I'm pretty sure that was a bona fide tease show, my little dove. These really are modern times."

"It wasn't *terrible*, I thought it rather daring. At the very least it was worth the price of admission," she said with a grin and a shiver of delight.

"I doubt the bluenose crowd would agree. It's only a matter of time before this show goes the way of the corner bar and the dodo bird." He took her arm and led her up the street. "At any rate, we absolutely must get doused before going to this party tonight. We don't want to be gauche enough to show up right when it begins. My eyes spy just the place to procure a little giggle juice."

"Can we get in?" Most speakeasies had a secret code or some other rigamarole one had to go through to get past the front door. Some were so well hidden you really had to be in the know to find them.

"Don't you worry about a thing, Pen. I have the keys to entry in my possession. Since this Prohibition mess started, I've been determined to visit each and every speakeasy in the city. I asked around about places near the Silver Palace, and let's just say my cup runneth over in this neighborhood. But this one is the closest."

Penelope followed the gesture he made with his hand toward a shoe repair shop that was inexplicably still lit up at this absurd hour of the night. They went through the motions of surreptitiously looking both ways before discreetly tapping on the door. After a moment, a small window at eye level opened. A pair of peepers peered out, studying the duo.

"One-two, buckle my shoe," Benny said with a wink.

The man grunted and opened the door for them. Inside, they were led past walls lined with shoes waiting to be repaired and straight to a door in the back. This wasn't a first for either of them so they squeezed into the tight space that was similar to many others that had been created out of any available nook and cranny. They ordered two cocktails, then found a spot to stand in the corner since there was no seating available.

"Don't get too blotto. I need you to be clear-headed enough to help me in my sleuthing at this party." Pen spoke in a hushed voice that was well-practiced over years of visiting other such secret establishments. After all, speakeasies had been named after the need to remain quiet so as not to alert the authorities.

"Pen, dove, it would take an ocean for me to get too blotto. I'm certain I've built up a tolerance by now, ironically enough thanks to Prohibition."

"I'm sure you have," she said with a quiet laugh as she sipped her mysterious cocktail. That was the fun thing about speakeasies, the curious concoctions different places came up with. Sometimes it seemed bartenders threw whatever they had on hand together and hoped it didn't turn out too terrible. The one she held was called a Honey Snapper. She could taste the honey and assumed the "snapper" was the bubbles from the ginger ale the liquor was mixed with. It was sweeter than she preferred but it was at least drinkable.

"So what am I on the hunt for tonight?" Benny asked with an overly alert expression, his dark eyes sparkling with delight. "What is this case you're working on?"

"If you promise not to gossip about it, I'll tell you."

"Pen, when have I ever gossiped?" he asked, highly offended.

She arched an eyebrow.

"Okay," he conceded, "but when have I ever broken a confidence?"

She lowered her lids and nodded in acknowledgment. Benny better than anyone knew how to keep a secret. "Okay then..."

Penelope told him everything. Unlike with Cousin Cordelia, she told the unvarnished truth, not having to worry about his nerves. She was pretty sure Benny's were made of steel...or maybe gin.

"Well, well," Benny hummed, sipping his drink as he considered everything she'd revealed. "So you think these thefts and his disappearance are related? That does make sense. Maybe whoever dug through Frank's things discovered something about him? Something he never showed his wife in the first place so she wouldn't even know if it was missing? So if we find the burglar, we may find out what happened to Jane's husband."

"Exactly, or at least get us much closer to the truth."

"Cheers to Agnes," he said, lifting his glass in honor of her. "The fun old girl got our Pen out of the gambling business and into something far more thrilling."

"Do you have any ideas?" she asked, not wanting to think about her old friend, whose death was still fresh in her memory.

"No, but I am a master at getting information," he said with a wicked grin. "These party-goers at Winchester Court have no idea what they are in for."

CHAPTER NINE

PENELOPE'S SECOND DRINK AT THE SPEAKEASY WASN'T as sweet as the first, but it was just as potent. By the time Benny and she spilled out onto the street to find a taxi, she was feeling rather ossified. She hoped the long drive up to the Upper West Side would help sober her up a bit.

She fell into Benny's side and he threw an arm around her, pulling her closer.

"I really do feel bad for Jane. Either Frank is dead or he's abandoned her. And he seemed like such a sweet husband, according to her."

"In which case, I fear it may be the worst, Pen."

"Yes," she agreed with a sigh. "But that doesn't explain the lie. Why wasn't he on that bus?"

"Perhaps he was protecting Jane from something. Is she the delicate type?"

"And then some. She's as naive as a lamb."

"Married to a wolf in sheep's clothing it would seem. Though some say all it takes is a good woman to change a bad man—in which case I'm doomed."

Penelope gave a tipsy laugh. "Maybe it worked. How much more virtuous can one be than a Bible salesman?"

Benny's laugh this time was somewhat harsher. "Oh dove, some of the worst transgressors I know are Bible peddlers. What better way to make people think you're a saint?"

Pen considered that for a moment. "Poor Jane."

Benny patted her on the shoulder and she dozed off for a while. It was the feel of him nudging her that had her awake again, feeling slightly more lucid after the long car ride.

"Come along Cinderella, the ball has only just begun!" Benny sang in a flamboyant manner as he escorted her out of the taxi and toward the entrance. "Look at us, we're both destined to be the belles of the ball."

Benny was being perfectly outrageous. Pen's gaze lifted to the windows on the second floor. The Middleberry's drapes were firmly closed, but Adam Pulley was once again staring out at the street below. Being that Daisy's party was the only action this time of night, his gaze was pinned on them. Once again Pen had the idea that he was studying them. He was a strange man indeed, and obviously a night owl.

Nearing them on the sidewalk, a trio of boisterous young women were practically skipping toward Winchester Court, obviously here for the same party. Penelope peered harder to see if she recognized them from the *Garden of Delights* and honestly couldn't tell. Then again, she, like most of the audience hadn't exactly been focused on their faces.

Benny and Pen made it to the front door before them and pressed the button for 2D.

"Are you here for Daisy's party too?" One of the trio of

girls asked as they waited for either someone to call or just come down and open the door. "I sure hope she keeps throwing these things when she becomes a Ziegfeld girl."

"*Ohh la la,*" sang one of them, making a pose before succumbing to laughter.

"Don't be sore, Lila. Good for Daisy making it big."

"The only thing big are the pockets of her fella."

They all laughed knowingly.

That explained a lot. Pen and Benny eyed each other. "Do any of you know who this fella is?" Penelope took a chance on asking.

The three looked at each other, then shrugged in unison.

"I'm pretty sure the point is we ain't supposed to know," Lila said with a smirk.

The door was opened by a flapper wearing a gold, beaded dress and holding a coupe glass containing something white and cloudy. "Come on in!"

Penelope and Benny allowed the other three to go ahead of them. They could hear the party down in the foyer. All of them followed it back up to Daisy's apartment. The door was already opened, which explained the noise. Somewhere inside, a victrola or radio was blaring music. That and the sound of laughter, talking, and even clinking glasses and bottles were enough to completely wake Penelope up.

As Benny and she shed their coats she noted that Daisy's apartment had the same layout as the Petersons', though it was a mirror image. Like their place, it was large and spacious, enough to hold the crowd of people which must have easily been about fifty or so.

Benny grabbed Penelope's hand and dragged her over to where the sound of clinking glass was the strongest. Daphne was set up at a standing bar making drinks, even though she looked half-blotto already. She wore another beaded sparkly number, tonight in red, with the same swanky shoes from that morning. So far, her dark bob was still neatly in place, tonight topped with a feathered headband.

"Hiya, Dahlia," she greeted Penelope with a giggle. "It's only champagne and White Ladies tonight. Which is your poison?"

That made sense. The champagne was probably in celebration of Daisy's career change, and the White Ladies were the perfect drink to describe her missing cat, which she had claimed this party was in honor of.

Penelope took a White Lady, knowing that the bubbles from the champagne would just go to her head. Benny of course had champagne, his favorite.

She watched as the woman poured crème de menthe, triple sec, and squeezed lemon juice into a shaker, then shook the whole thing. With an ice pick, she stabbed away at a large block of ice and added a few chunks. She shook again before straining the whole thing into a glass.

"Well if it isn't our little Dahlia!" Penelope turned around at the sound of Spanky's voice and saw him approaching. He was wearing almost the same thing she'd seen him in this morning, though looking less disheveled...so far.

"So you've decided to come to Daisy's little farewell shindig," Spanky said, his eyes trained on Penelope with a tinge of amusement.

"Is this her last party?"

"Heaven's no, at least I hope not! But this weekend is to be our amazing Daisy's last performance in *mon magnifique jardin. Ce ne sera pas pareil sans elle.*"

Penelope had of course taken French in school, but it

had been a while since she had spoken it with anyone. Still, she understood what Spanky had said. Apart from lamenting his magnificent garden, he'd commented that it wouldn't be the same without Daisy.

"Yes, yes, she's the star of the show," Daphne said, smirking and rolling her eyes as she poured Benny's champagne.

"Benny and I saw *Garden of Delights* tonight. It was... interesting."

Daphne and Spanky both laughed.

"I do believe that is the quaintest description I've ever heard about our little darling of a show," Spanky mused.

"Though maybe now with Daisy gone, we can get away from flowers? Or at least I can be a rose. Everyone knows red is my color," Daphne suggested.

Penelope thought back to Daphne's performance. It had been a little number involving some strategically placed gaudy purple bouquets. She was probably sick of it by now.

"I suppose we'll have to. Though that doesn't solve all our problems," Spanky said with a long sigh.

He brightened up when he realized the three of them were staring.

"Not to worry, Spanky always has a plan for resurrection!"

"What is Spanky short for?" Penelope asked, just for confirmation.

"That is a secret I shall take to the grave," he said, touching the side of his nose.

"Spencer Ankara," Daphne said, rolling her eyes again. "He just likes to be mysterious."

Spanky frowned at her, but it was too exaggerated to be taken seriously. "Daphne, you'll ruin the mystique!"

"It's right there on the poster, you egg."

That at least confirmed he was the one who had written and produced the *Garden of Delights*. Now with Daisy gone, perhaps he was worried about the show's success? Maybe enough to need a second source of income, like robbing an apartment building where he knew the residents had money, and thus valuables?

"How often does Daisy throw these parties?" Penelope asked.

"Every night she performs, that's Thursday through Sunday, if you ever want to come to an encore. Of course, she isn't always free to play the hostess, if you catch my drift. At least not for us mere mortals," he said with a wink.

"Are you suggesting something of the sugar variety?" Benny asked with pursed lips. "Who do you suppose supplies it?"

"JD?" Spanky replied with a shrug. "That one truly is a mystery."

"He must have loads if he can afford this place," Daphne said, looking around.

"At any rate, I just arrived and have yet to thank our hostess," Spanky said before offering a silly bow and leaving.

Penelope and Benny got out of the way of the bar as several attendees approached for drinks.

"What do you think?" Penelope asked.

"I do know he's no, *ahem*, daisy."

"What?"

"He couldn't keep his eyes off you, Pen. And all when I'm looking so handsome," he pouted. "Not that I blame him, you look gorgeous in that dress."

"Maybe Daisy just assumed something of him because he's in the theater?"

"He does have a certain flair for the dramatic, but no.

Honestly, I wouldn't be surprised if he's sown the entire garden with his plow, if you catch what I mean," he said with a smirk.

"*Benny*," Penelope said with a laugh, elbowing him. "At any rate, let's separate and mingle. We might as well take advantage while we're here. See if anyone is a frequent guest at these parties. Ask if they know anything about the neighbors or these robberies."

"Aye, captain," Benny said, saluting her.

She grinned and wandered off. While she circled the room she studied the interior of Daisy's apartment. It was modern but in an unabashedly feminine manner. The curtains were done in a gauzy rose, slightly darker than the soft baby pink of the walls. The furniture was mostly white, with fluffs of pillows strewn about. No man lived here that was for certain.

As the night wore on, she learned little of value. Most of the guests were frequent attendees, and no one knew who Daisy's secret benefactor was. As far as she could tell, everyone here was somehow involved with the theater, and just as much on the nut as the average performer would be. This meant they all had motive and opportunity to steal from the other residents.

Still, a zozzled flapper was bound to draw some attention if she went about breaking into people's apartments, then trying to escape. Penelope thought back to what Daphne and Spanky looked like this morning. The idea of either of them making a run for it, their arms stuffed with jewelry and furs—not to mention a silver button and whatever else was in that box that Frank didn't want Jane to know about—made her laugh out loud.

She really needed to take it easy on the White Ladies.

At some point, the cigarette smoke and heat from the

crowd forced her toward the window, which was cracked open to let in some of the chilly air outside. Like Jane's apartment, Daisy's faced the back. This time of night she couldn't see a thing, being that the back didn't have the benefit of street lights. Even in the dim light from the apartments of the few people who were up this late, she could barely make out the dead plants let alone the fence.

Pen sipped and turned back to watch the crowd. She caught a glimpse of Daisy, who she hadn't been able to greet yet. The hostess looked perfectly dour tonight. Even the joyous crowd around her couldn't force a begrudging smile to her face. The loss of her cat must have really upset her. A crease formed in her brow and she nibbled her bottom lip as she stared down into her drink.

Penelope thought about walking over to console her but Spanky reached her first. Rather than be comforted by his appearance it only seemed to irritate her. She shook off the hand he rested on her shoulder and said something that had his head jerking back, as though in surprise.

I wonder what that's about...

"How do you do it, Benny? I don't think I can even stand for another minute," Penelope protested. It was almost four in the morning and she had reached her limit as far as the party went.

"The key is to pace yourself, Pen. Sleeping until noon the day before also helps."

She laughed tiredly. "Did you learn anything new?"

Daisy had disappeared to her bedroom, never to be seen again. She had looked just as miserable then as she had when Pen had caught her snapping at Spanky.

"Only that I definitely need to spend more time with dancers and flappers. They're so much fun! Otherwise, no. None of the girls knows who John Keyes or Key might be. No one knows anything about the Petersons at all. No one knows who this mysterious JD is. Everyone misses Lady, who was *just the sweetest thing*. And each of them is hoping to be the new Daisy in the show. Except..." he paused to consider something. "A lot of them think maybe the show won't go on too long after Daisy leaves."

"Daisy was *that* essential to its success?"

"It seems so."

Penelope considered that. Daisy was certainly attractive and knew how to put on a show, but in New York, there were a thousand young women just as pretty and just as lacking in inhibition. This was a city where sinners came to play.

At any rate, she also hadn't learned much that would help her with Jane's case. Frank Peterson was just as much a mystery tonight—or rather this morning—as he was the day before.

"I'm going to breeze," Penelope said, hugging him. "After all, I'm a working woman now and I've got to come back later on to try a different plan of attack."

Mostly, she wanted to press Jane for any more details about Frank's past. She also wanted a more thorough look through his box, just in case she'd missed something. That did seem to be the key to it all.

She quickly finished the last of the White Lady in her cup, briefly noting how it wouldn't help the morning's certain hangover, and then she bloused.

The night was even more blisteringly cold in the wee hours of the morning. Penelope realized she'd have to walk to the nearest avenue if she hoped to catch a taxi. As she walked she turned back to look at Winchester Court. Although Adam Pulley's light was out, his curtains were open and she swore she could feel his eyes watching her as she went.

"Zounds," she grumbled. Between him and Mrs. Middleberry covering the daytime, they could probably put your average spy to shame in terms of catching anything. It was a wonder how any burglar got away with the goods.

Either way, Adam Pulley was going to the top of her list of suspects.

But first, she needed a good sleep to sober up.

CHAPTER TEN

THE NEXT MORNING, PENELOPE FELT MISERABLE. IF she never saw another White Lady, she'd be perfectly fine with that—whether it was the drink or the darn cat.

As she joined Cousin Cordelia for a late Saturday morning breakfast, she thought about Daisy and how pitiful she looked last night. Perhaps it wouldn't be such a bad thing if Pen also discovered who had taken her beloved cat while she was discovering what happened to Frank Peterson.

However, the thought of getting fully dressed and making the trip across town to the west side only made the carpenters in her head hammer that much harder.

"Penelope dear, you look a travesty."

"Thank you, Cousin Cordelia," she deadpanned.

"I do hope you aren't coming down with something. This is the season for so many ailments. I suspect it's going to snow any day now, I can feel it in my bones."

"Lovely," Penelope said idly as she poured herself a cup of coffee.

Sally entered the library, where they took their breakfast at their usual table. She was carrying a tray holding a tall glass filled with something red.

"I see you've started working already, thank heavens," Penelope observed, feeling somewhat mortified about her condition. Sally probably thought she was some feckless chippy who did nothing but drink, party, and squander the money she'd been left. Suddenly Pen regretted being so cavalier during her informal interview.

"I hope it isn't too forward of me, but I thought this might help with your..." she cast a quick glance toward Cousin Cordelia. "ailment. One of my prior employers was often afflicted and introduced me to this solution that he learned of in Paris. It's a mix of tomato juice, vodka, and a few other ingredients," she said with a conspiratorial smile.

"It sounds perfectly dreadful," Cousin Cordelia remarked. "But then homemade remedies usually are. Alas, the price we pay for good health."

It did sound awful, but something about Sally's professional bonhomie made Penelope trust it. Frankly, she would have tried anything at this point.

"Thank you, Sally," Penelope said accepting the drink, which for some silly reason had a celery stalk in it. Was she supposed to eat that as well for it to work? Perhaps it was just decoration. She'd seen the oddest things thrown into cocktails these days. It was as if Prohibition gave people a license to be perfectly frivolous. "What do you call this concoction?"

Sally paused as though in thought. "I'm sorry, miss, I don't seem to recall." She cast another glance toward Cousin Cordelia, which made Penelope think she was just being considerate of her older cousin's sensitivities.

Taking into account the red coloring of the drink, Penelope could hazard a few guesses as to what creative and perfectly macabre name the inventor had given it. Still, she drank. It wasn't half as bad as she thought it would be.

Penelope satisfied herself with some scrambled eggs and a single strip of bacon as she switched between coffee and the tomato-vodka drink. By the time she had finished, she almost felt herself again. The "solution" had worked wonders in that regard.

"I think Sally will do smashingly," she said brightly as she smiled out at Central Park through the windows. Even the dreary gray sky did nothing to dampen her recovering mood at this point.

Frankly, she thought Sally deserved a raise for not only being perfectly nonjudgemental about Penelope's nocturnal escapades and the consequences the morning after, but for being an ally in helping her recover.

"Oh, I do hope so. She seems to understand almost intuitively when I need my medicine."

Penelope was certain of that. Hopefully, Sally limited it to mere understanding and not indulgence. They'd had to let their last maid go for getting caught completely blotto, holding an empty bottle of Cousin Cordelia's "medicine."

It was almost noon by the time Penelope arrived back at the Winchester Court apartments. She pushed the button for Jane's apartment and waited for her voice. Through the decorative ironwork covering the glass front door, she could see Daisy at the mailboxes, slipping an envelope into the outgoing slot. Rather than wait for Jane to call down, she knocked to get her attention.

Daisy jumped, startled, and turned to frown at the door. When she saw it was Penelope, her expression softened. Still, Penelope could see how wretched she looked. The silk robe she had on hung off one shoulder, and she was barefoot. She slowly walked over to open the door for her. Up close, her pretty face was puffy and splotched as though she'd been crying all morning. She hadn't bothered to put on a hint of makeup or comb her hair.

"Goodness Daisy, you poor thing. Are you still worried about Lady?"

Daisy sniffed and stared at Penelope in wonder before shaking her head as though shaking free a coherent thought. "Yes, of course. She's still gone. I only wish..."

"Come on," Penelope said, resting an arm around her shoulder and gently guiding her back upstairs. The last thing Daisy needed was any hassle from neighbors who might pass by. They probably already thought she was problematic.

On the second floor, a woman was lugging a device off the elevator. Both Daisy and the woman stopped short, each stiffening in surprise as they caught sight of each other.

"Oh, hello Ana," Daisy said tightly.

This must have been Ana Klukovich, wife of the man in charge of maintenance. She was older, about twice Daisy's age, and the dour and slightly haggard look on her face only added years. She simply nodded, without offering any hint of a smile as she plugged in the device. That must have been the carpet sweeper to which Mrs. Middleberry had been referring.

She cast a brief suspicious glance Penelope's way before she turned the machine on. Penelope jumped at the sound of it. They'd been around for years now, but she'd never heard one this up close before.

Zounds, no wonder Mrs. Middleberry complained!

Pen quickly guided Daisy back through her door, which she'd left unlocked. Even with it firmly closed, she could hear the dull sound of that contraption as Ana guided it back and forth along the carpeted hallway.

This late in the day, even the stragglers had left the party, leaving behind nothing but an apartment that looked as though a tornado had swept through it.

"Ana's always runnin' that thing," Daisy said dully. "She don't like me very much. Nobody does."

"That's not true," Penelope reassured her. "Look how many people came to your party last night."

Daisy snorted and fell onto her sofa. "They just wanna see me fail. You have no idea how nasty people can be, even when you're at your worst. Even those closest to you will betray you."

Penelope had a pretty good idea of how nasty people could be. The three years she had essentially been a pariah among the New York elite, she knew full well the gossip about her never ceased.

"Do you have any coffee? Tea?"

Daisy wailed. "I don't want coffee or tea! I just want Lady. She's the only one who really loves me. Not Jameson or the girls or even Spanky."

Penelope swallowed, wondering if Daisy knew how much she had just revealed. Was Jameson the J in JD whom Spanky had mentioned last night?

Daisy seemed to realize a fraction too late what she'd revealed. She gave a Pen bashful smile. "Oops, I guess the cat is out of the bag, isn't it?"

Perhaps it was the mention of the word "cat," but a moment later she was bawling.

"What does it matter? Whoever took Lady already knows anyway. They found my diary, even though I had it locked up and well hidden. It's all over."

"Has he ended things with you?"

Daisy sniffed, collecting herself. She wiped her eyes with the back of her hand and frowned. "Yeah. That's why I was sending a letter, trying to win him back. But that don't matter, I can make it on my own!" The momentary bit of verve that statement gave her, chin lifted a bit higher, immediately deflated as reality sunk in. "I think I can, anyways. I just wish Lady was here. She always made me feel better."

Pen realized she needed to delicately extract herself from this situation otherwise she'd be here all day consoling Daisy. She owed it to Jane to get back to the case of Frank Peterson. Still, she couldn't just leave Daisy like this.

"Why don't I try looking for her? I'm pretty good at this sort of thing." She didn't want to reveal her profession, lest she find herself officially hired for a second case. She was hardly making headway on the first one as it was.

"You'd do that for me?" Daisy asked, looking so much like a little girl that Penelope wanted to hug her. At least when Penelope was at her worst, she'd still had Cousin Cordelia and Agnes Sterling there for her.

"Of course. Maybe the thief didn't take her and she's just hiding out somewhere?" That was most likely the case. It didn't make sense to steal furs, stocks, and then a cat.

"Thank you, Penelope," Daisy said, softly. "You're the bee's knees."

Penelope smiled and made her goodbyes.

Thankfully, Ana had left the floor with her noisy machine. As she passed by the stairs leading down to the foyer, she saw Ana exiting a side door labeled, "Maintenance Only." That must have been where she stored the carpet sweeper. She saw Penelope staring and the scowl that she shot her was perfectly venomous. It was quite obvious that Daisy was persona non grata in this building, and Penelope was feeling the effects of that by proximity.

Penelope quickly walked on. She had planned to go to each floor and do a quick look just to search for any white cat hairs. Of course, Ana and her sweeper had made that idea moot. Still, Daisy had said something about a cat in 3C that Lady liked to play with. It wouldn't hurt just to quickly ask if the owner had seen Lady recently.

She knocked and waited. After a moment, the door opened a crack. Penelope could see that the chain was still on as a woman looked out with a suspicious gaze.

"Hello," Penelope said, planting an ingratiating smile on her face. "I'm sorry to bother you but—"

Before she could explain her reason for knocking she heard a sharp yowl and something orange and furry squeezed through the crack and down the hall.

"*Pumpkin*!"

The cat continued, racing toward the end and coming to a stop, looking around, and then came back again. It detoured toward the window that led out to the fire escape. Upon finding it closed, it let out another yowl, sounding perfectly vexed. The poor thing was probably tired of being cooped up inside all winter.

"Oh," the woman cried, slamming the door to release the chain then throwing it open again. "You come back here you naughty, naughty thing you! It's wintertime, silly, I can't let you out to play today."

Pumpkin was almost the size of a large pumpkin, especially compared to the slight woman who took hold of the cat. She glared at Penelope as though this was her fault.

"Beautiful cat," she offered, forcing a smile and hoping that would curry some favor.

The woman smiled, then pouted down at Pumpkin. "At least we didn't pee everywhere this time, did we, sweetums? You know how much mumsy dislikes that," she said in a cloying voice.

Pumpkin simply hissed in response.

Penelope took a step back. If this was Lady's playmate, it was no wonder she had disappeared.

"I was just wondering if lately you'd seen a white-haired Persian cat? Lady, she belongs to—"

"I know exactly the cat to which you are referring," the woman said curtly, her eyes narrowing at Pen. "She did nothing but cause trouble, leaving my poor sweet Pumpkin in a perfect state! A bad influence is what she was, and no, I haven't seen her in weeks and both Pumpkin and I are all the better for it!"

She closed the door firmly in Penelope's face before she could inquire further. On the other side, she could hear the mix of a yowling Pumpkin and a sweet-talking owner.

It seemed both Lady and Daisy were unwanted creatures at Winchester Court. Penelope felt bad for both of them. All the same, it was clear that 3C certainly hadn't taken Lady.

It was also clear that Penelope was leading herself down a rabbit hole. At this point, she felt like Alice in Wonderland, only instead of chasing a white rabbit, she was chasing a white cat!

"Zounds," she muttered to herself. She took a breath and headed downstairs to finally meet with Jane again.

Pen knocked on Jane's door, with no answer.

Behind her, she heard 2A's door opening and sighed as she braced herself.

"She still hasn't come back," Mrs. Middleberry said. Penelope turned to find her lips pursed with disapproval. "She spent the night *elsewhere*."

"Did she?" Penelope asked indifferently. Her mind, however, was awhirl with questions and concerns, none of which would be expressed to Mrs. Middleberry.

"Has her husband returned yet?" The implication was

evident. Mrs. Middleberry seemed to think that Jane had decided to spend the night with another man since her husband was gone.

"Oh! Silly me," Penelope feigned, pressing her palm to her head. "I completely forgot that Jane mentioned going to visit with her sick aunt last night."

Mrs. Middleberry seemed reluctant to let go of her suppositions, but she couldn't very well call Penelope a liar. "Oh, well.... Still, it *is* odd she only took her purse with her?"

That was odd, especially for being gone overnight.

"She probably didn't expect to stay the night. Her aunt...*Cordelia* is nearly at the end. She must have taken a turn for the worse."

Pen hoped the grave expression on her face would end this. When Mrs. Middleberry leaned in, eager for more, she realized she needed to escape.

"In fact, I should go visit myself before it's too late. Offer my condolences and all."

She hurried off, quickly taking the stairs down. She slowed down once in the privacy of the foyer to process the news that Jane was still gone.

From what little she had learned about her, Jane wasn't the type to simply leave and spend the night elsewhere. The Petersons didn't even socialize with their own neighbors. So where the devil was she?

Pen could only assume the worst.

"Curiouser and curiouser," she muttered to herself with dread and frustration.

Her eyes fell on the door that Ana had exited earlier, the one marked "Maintenance Only." Perhaps her reaction to Pen hadn't been about Daisy, but instead about what was hidden on the other side of that door?

Mrs. Middleberry had indicated that the police had cleared the Klukovichs of theft, even searching their apartment. But had the police checked every place to which they had access?

Penelope felt her heart quicken with excitement. Could it be as easy as this? She quickly raced over and tried the door handle. She wasn't surprised to find it was locked.

Of all the illicit activities she had become embroiled in during her colorful past, picking locks was not one of them. Odd considering some of the more tricky situations she had found herself in. It certainly would have come in handy right now.

She wasn't about to try her hand at it only to have some resident come traipsing down the stairs to catch her in the act. Or worse, Mrs. Klukovich, who might then realize Penelope was on to her.

"Pineapples," Penelope cursed to herself. It was her standard substitute for a curse word that she had taken to using since she was a little girl, one who didn't want to get into even more trouble than she already had.

The door and whatever was behind it would have to wait for another day. Penelope exited into the cold February air. The sky was still gloomy. Perhaps Cousin Cordelia was right about eventual snow. Still, she considered going for a walk. The cold air had a way of invigorating her.

Instead, her eye caught the corner cafe where she had bought Detective Prescott's lunch. She decided a cup of coffee would work just as well for helping her think this all out.

CHAPTER ELEVEN

Penelope sat at a small table by the window of the cafe near Winchester Court. From this vantage point, she had a perfect view of the apartment building. Perhaps if she sat here long enough she'd catch Jane finally returning from wherever she was.

Pen frowned thinking about Jane. Mrs. Middleberry had said she'd left in a hurry, but that didn't mean much. Anyone would quicken their step at the prospect of being cornered by that obtrusive woman. Still, to leave and not come back all night?

"By yourself today? Will it be another coffee and eggs?"

Penelope turned around in surprise, wondering if that was being addressed to her.

The waitress gave a small, apologetic laugh. "I'm sorry, I thought you were someone else who lives in the neighborhood. Can I get you something?"

"I'll take that cup of coffee, but instead with some apple pie if you have it today. Is it hot?"

"We can certainly warm it up for you. Nice day for it, isn't it?"

"Perfect," Penelope said with a smile.

After the waitress left, Penelope stared out the window in thought about what she'd learned today.

Daisy was somehow involved with a "Jameson" who was no doubt paying for her to live in this very nice neighborhood. Whoever had taken Lady and Daisy's other valuables had somehow also discovered who Jameson was, most likely from her diary.

Perhaps they had tried to blackmail him? Maybe that was why it was over between him and Daisy. A mistress was only worth the risk if the relationship remained discreet and unproblematic. Exposure negated both of those.

Whoever this thief was, they certainly had a knack for using information. Anyone smart enough knew that information could be far more valuable than furs or jewelry.

So what had they learned about Frank? Did it have to do with what was taken from that box? Was it just as, if not more valuable than what they'd learned about Daisy's affair?

It was slowly coming together now.

"All because of a missing cat," Penelope whispered to herself with a humorless laugh.

Now she felt she owed it to Lady to discover her whereabouts.

"Here you are, nice and hot," the waitress said, bringing back a steaming cup of coffee and a plate with a warm slice of golden apple pie.

Penelope wasted no time tucking into it, momentarily dismissing her case in favor of savoring something warm and delicious.

She was halfway through her pie and just about to ask for a refill of her coffee when she saw a familiar face walking out the front door of Winchester Court.

Adam Pulley.

He tightened his scarf around his neck and turned in the opposite direction, continuing down the street.

Penelope took two seconds to decide what to do. A moment later, she was out of her seat, pie unfinished. She dug into her purse and grabbed a five-dollar bill. It was significantly more than the cost of what she'd ordered but she handed it off to the waitress without waiting for change. Why not make her day with a fat tip?

Pen rushed out of the cafe and hurried along until she caught sight of Adam ahead of her. He was casually strolling toward Amsterdam Avenue, where he turned, heading north.

She wasn't sure what she was after by following him, maybe just an idea of who the man was. Where was he heading this chilly Saturday afternoon? He didn't seem to be in search of a taxi which hopefully meant he wasn't going too far. Penelope hadn't exactly worn the proper shoes to ankle it around town. At least her coat was warm enough, and if she pulled her hat down firmly her ears were covered.

Fortunately, he came to a stop at 82nd Street and crossed there. Penelope stayed back to watch him, hiding among the few people brave enough to face the cold. After crossing Amsterdam, he continued a short way, stopping to enter a three-story building.

Penelope followed his path until she too was in front of the building, which turned out to be a branch of the New York Public Library.

That took the wind out of her sails some. Pen wasn't sure what she had been hoping for. Perhaps a nondescript building where he'd be meeting with a secret society of professional thieves?

Penelope breathed out a laugh. The fog that appeared in front of her was a reminder of how cold it was. She might as well go inside to warm up for a bit.

Once inside, she wandered, idly looking for Adam while pretending to scan the bookshelves. She didn't find him in the mostly open area of the first floor, so she casually ascended the stairs to the second floor and did the same. She almost revealed herself when she turned a corner to head to the next row of books.

Adam was there, perusing the shelves. Penelope waited, deciding she'd stay long enough to see what subject was so interesting to him, if only out of curiosity. She whiled the time away, scanning the shelf in front of her that held books on...children and childcare?

"Find what you were looking for?"

Penelope jumped at the sound of his voice. She turned and found Adam Pulley standing at the end of the row. He greeted her with that same mild smile he'd offered when he caught her staring at Winchester Court from the street yesterday.

"I, um," she said, hurriedly grabbing a book off the shelf just to look innocent. "Do I recognize you? You look familiar."

His smile broadened. "Come now, Miss Banks, let's not maintain the facade. Why not have a seat and I can help you piece together what it is you're after?"

"I..." Her brow wrinkled with bewilderment. How did he know her name? Was this some ruse to confuse her or perhaps throw her off his scent?

"Ah, I can see the problem. It is wise to make introductions first, no? I'm Adam Pulley, but I'm going to guess that Mrs. Middleberry probably already revealed that piece of information. She is quite the treasure trove, is she not? As for how I know your name, well, I must confess to being a sort of snoop myself—an occupational idiosyncrasy."

"She did mention that you were an author. Would I find any of your work here?"

He laughed softly. "You might—under another name of course."

Someone on the floor shushed them.

In a lowered voice he continued. "Perhaps we could take this conversation elsewhere. There's a small restaurant across the street I often eat at during my ventures outside. Allow me to check out my materials and we can enjoy a late lunch while we work on what it is that has brought you to Winchester Court. I'm guessing it's one of two, perhaps three things."

Penelope didn't automatically agree. Adam Pulley seemed harmless enough, and lunch at a public place hardly posed a danger, other than someone assuming certain things about the two of them. He was almost old enough to be her father, but that would only make the assumption seem more sordid.

Still, for Daisy's and Jane's sakes, she would agree.

"Fine," she said, shoving the book back on the shelf and following him down to the first floor—at a firm distance.

Pen made sure to take note of the two books Mr. Pulley checked out. One was on the rules of cricket, and the other was on making cheese. Neither topic, as obscure as they were, did anything to alleviate her suspicion. Still, she doubted any of her other suspects would be so accommodating.

After Adam checked out his books, he jauntily led her outside and across the street to a German restaurant.

Once they were seated he exhaled a small chuckle. "I can remember the days when such things were not done, a young, single woman going out unaccompanied to a restaurant with a strange man. There is something to be said for progress. War does have a modernizing effect on culture."

"Did you serve?"

"In the Great War? No, I was recruited to join a far more obscure little spat with our neighbors to the south, being that I have a flair for languages. But I have studied it at great length; the war that will end war they said. I have my doubts. That treaty President Wilson signed over there in Versailles did no one any favors. But then, that's hardly the least of his failings is it?"

Penelope had no interest in politics or talk of war. Fortunately, the waiter came by to take their drink orders.

"Such a shame one can no longer order a nice glass of beer with their bauernwurst," he lamented after the waiter left.

"Mr. Pulley—"

"Adam, please. I think we can dispense with all the formalities."

Penelope didn't bother wasting time to protest. "Adam. What is it you think I'm after?"

"Let's select our entrees first, shall we? I hate to pontificate on an empty stomach."

Penelope sighed with impatience and looked at the menu. She decided the schnitzel was satisfactory. Adam seemed to already have his favorite and they quickly dispensed with ordering.

"Now, as to what it is I think you're after?" He stroked his chin in thought, once again looking like a professor. "I know you came to Winchester to visit Jane Peterson. You then somehow allowed Mrs. Middleberry to lure you into her web, a fate from which the average person would normally try to escape. This leads me to believe you are seeking information."

"You really are quite the busybody," she remarked not bothering to hide her criticism.

He laughed. "I like to study people is all. I'm a perpetual student of human behavior. That is why I selected Winchester Court. It's a rather interesting building, wouldn't you agree?"

"How so?"

"Let's just say it makes it very convenient for people who enjoy their privacy. No doorman keeping watch over your comings and goings. Very few residents on each floor, very few in the entire building in fact, at least compared to other modern apartment buildings in New York. A convenient call system so people know who is coming to visit. One has to be let in by the resident they are there to see, though that system is flawed, as you've no doubt noticed. Still, a certain type of individual is drawn to a building like that. I have a theory that every resident has a secret they'd like to maintain, or at least some very good reason why they want a private life."

"And what is *your* secret?"

He laughed good-naturedly. "I suppose I invited that question. What do you think it is?"

"That you like to rob your neighbors of their valuables?" Penelope offered in a dry tone, making him laugh again.

"That's another thing about Winchester Court residents, most of us are very well off. If you knew how much the rent was, you'd understand that."

"Maybe some of them are simply keeping up appearances?" she offered, giving him a pointed look.

"That may in fact be the case," he said with a subtle

smile. "As for myself, I confess I am indeed quite well off, rich even."

"So you claim."

"Alright," he said, considering her. "I'll offer to tell you my secret if you offer to tell me what your interest in Winchester Court, or rather the Petersons, is."

"I'm not in the habit of violating the confidence of my friends."

"Hmm," he said nodding. "That is wise. How about instead, I'll tell you what I think it is, and you can agree or disagree?"

"That doesn't give you much leverage."

"This is simply a fun little lark for me. It will help me with my work."

"Which is...? What is it exactly that you write?"

"Does the name Abner Ellis strike a chord?"

Penelope's mouth fell open. "The mystery author?"

He simply nodded.

"But that's...how many books?"

"Forty so far, and that's just one of my pen names. I have three in total."

"How ever do you find time to sleep?"

"As you've no doubt noticed, I don't get much. I prefer small naps throughout the day and night. Otherwise, you can usually find me studying up on a subject," he patted the books next to him, "or writing. I have a craft for story-telling."

"In other words lying?"

He smiled begrudgingly. "Yes, my imagination is quite robust. It comes in handy in solving crimes, though mostly of the imaginary kind."

"What does it tell you about who might have committed the burglaries in your building?"

"I'm surprised you don't suspect me."

"I do."

He laughed. "A smart thing. But no, Miss Banks, I'm afraid it isn't me."

"That's exactly what the culprit would say."

He laughed again. Penelope found it disarming, causing her to relax somewhat. It was rare to spend time with someone who seemed to find life so lighthearted and amusing but was also intellectual.

That certainly didn't mean she was going to dismiss him as the culprit.

"I'm a rather obvious suspect, aren't I? I'm there most of the day and night. I have a window that overlooks the front entrance so I know when my neighbors have left. No doubt Mrs. Middleberry has told you about my habit of walking the hallways and stairs. I am otherwise a complete mystery. Perhaps I'm not, in fact, the author behind Abner Ellis as I claim to be?"

"You're not helping clear yourself of suspicion."

"No, I suppose I'm not. But to help clear my good name, I beg you to contact my publishing house. Provide your name and ask them about me. I'll permit them to divulge the truth."

"That's awfully accommodating of you."

"I find you interesting."

Penelope sat back warily.

He laughed. "No, no, not in that manner. I'm not... *inclined* that way. Something you're familiar with, I believe? Though, I tend to be slightly less...*expressive* about it than your friend. You don't have to concern yourself as far as that goes, Miss Banks."

"Penelope," she offered, relaxing a bit more. He really was a good study of humans. Penelope hadn't figured out her friend Benny was *inclined* that way until they were adults.

Adam gave a brief nod. "Penelope it is."

"Have you had anything stolen?"

He shook his head no. "I wouldn't make a very convenient target, frankly. I don't stick to a schedule or leave my apartment very often. I suppose that makes me the number one suspect?"

It did, but as he said it was also a little too obvious. He'd have to be the dumbest criminal on earth to target everyone on his floor, and not at least *pretend* to have some of his valuables stolen as well. Adam Pulley didn't strike her as stupid. "It would help ease my suspicion if you could tell me what you knew about the other residents."

He offered a wry smile realizing she was using him for information. "Should I start with Jane Peterson? Or perhaps that husband of hers you're in search of?"

Penelope tried to maintain an impassive expression, but couldn't prevent her jaw from working slightly. "What do you know about them?"

"Not much, and that in and of itself says something."

"Well, that's helpful," she said in a dry voice.

He laughed softly. "Yes, some people are very private, and perhaps that couple is a perfect example. Still, he must be quite the salesman with those Bibles of his. I wonder where he keeps them when he isn't traveling? Usually, salesmen travel with a trunk or suitcase of their wares."

"He doesn't keep them in the apartment?"

"I've never seen him with such a case. He takes off near the beginning of each month and then returns almost a week later, all with nothing more than a small suitcase. I assume *that* is filled with his change of clothes."

"So you don't think he sells Bibles?"

"I'd hate to risk damnation by condemning one of God's flock, *if* indeed he is the virtuous Bible salesman he claims he is."

Penelope's twist of the lips matched the tone of his voice. "Then what is it he does during his week away?"

"You're the detective. At least I presume?"

Penelope smiled but didn't confirm.

Their food conveniently arrived. By the time their plates were served, she decided not to directly answer his query, if only to protect Jane's privacy. Instead, she wanted to focus on the thefts, since she was almost certain they were related.

"It is odd that only the second floor suffered a bout of burglaries, don't you think?"

Adam grinned at her deliberate deflection. "Perhaps the thief is working their way up from the bottom to the top? The second floor is the most convenient to escape from."

"Most people commit crimes in places that are familiar to them, don't they?"

"On the other hand, a good thief would be smart enough to create at least some distance to allay any suspicion."

"Unless it's trickery. You're a detective author. It's always the least likely suspect, no?"

"Reality is a different animal. The most simple solution is often the answer. However, you do make a point about people being inclined to start at home. In that case, we have yours truly, the lovely Daisy and her cadre of partiers, Mr. & Mrs. Middleberry, and finally the Petersons."

"What do you know about the Klukovichs?"

"Ah yes, I forgot about *the help*. But that would be akin to laying blame on the butler no? How cliché."

"As you said, reality is a different animal. They would

be obvious suspects. They have plenty of opportunity and motive. I assume they have master keys to get them into any apartment and a reason for being on any floor at a given time. It can't be enjoyable catering to a building filled with rich, needy, entitled people. Why not avail oneself? Perhaps they also have a secret?"

"I'm almost certain of it."

"*What*?" Penelope had been facetious in the suggestion.

Adam simply cut into his steak and took a bite.

Penelope stared, waiting for him to explain that comment.

He sighed and set down his fork and knife. "Now I am the one beholden to maintain a confidence, or rather, an unfair aspersion."

"If it's related to the crime then surely—"

Adam put up one hand to silence her. "I will tell you some of it if you'll promise to keep it in strict confidence unless you are absolutely sure it's related to a crime they've committed."

Penelope thought about it and nodded her head. "*Only* if I don't think it's related."

He nodded. "The Klukovichs haven't always been 'the help,' so to speak. In fact, I'd gather they were probably once wealthier than anyone currently residing at Winchester Court."

Penelope blinked in surprise. "Really?"

"From St. Petersburg. I take it you're at least somewhat familiar with what happened in Russia several years ago?"

Of course Penelope had heard about the Tsar and his family, as well as the revolution surrounding their assassinations. The Bolsheviks had eventually taken over, causing many people to flee Russia.

"Fortunes have a way of changing," Adam said. Penelope offered a sad, ironic smile at that. "I think the Klukoviches feel lucky to be alive. Many members of the aristocracy didn't make it out of Russia. They escaped with only the clothes on their backs."

"I thought most of them immigrated to France or other places in Europe?"

"Yes, yes, the *White Emigré*," he said. "I met a few when I spent several months in Paris after the war. Most did stay in Europe, but there was a segment drawn here to the land of the free. Today, I'm sure they wished they had made a different choice. Unfortunately, many Americans cast a suspicious eye on any Russian immigrant, even those who have every reason to be vehemently opposed to the Bolsheviks."

"So, as I said, perhaps they resent their circumstances?" Penelope suggested. "Maybe they'd like to live the way they once did?"

He pierced her with his gaze. "And if you find definitive proof that they did something illegal, I would be the first to encourage you to follow through with gusto."

Penelope thought about that door marked "Maintenance Only." Adam had offered nothing that supported Ana Klukovich's innocence. Until Pen had a look beyond that door, the couple would remain on her list of suspects.

"Onto the next person on your list," Adam said brightly as he returned to his steak.

"Well, Daisy has too many friends to even think about considering. It could be any one of the people who attend her parties."

Adam nodded in agreement. "Yes, it could."

"As for the Middleberrys, well, they are just so..."

"Harmless?" he finished for her with a chuckle. "Don't let that deceive you."

"Do you suspect something of them?"

"As I said, everyone in the building has secrets."

Penelope wondered if he knew something about them and was just toying with her. "Do *they*?"

"To be fair, I've never found them interesting enough to investigate. That doesn't mean anything. Crime can be perfectly boring at its heart. No genius mastermind at the helm, just basic greed, envy, wrath, and so on and so forth."

"That isn't exactly a vote of confidence for them."

"If you happen to find something interesting, I'd be curious to know."

Penelope gave him a wry smile and continued eating. She was enjoying herself. It was nice to have an intelligent person to discuss this with, someone who was as curious about things as she was.

"And me? Do you still consider me a suspect?" Adam asked with an inquiring look.

"Of course," Penelope said in a perfectly frank tone.

Adam lifted his glass and laughed. "I'd be disappointed if you didn't."

CHAPTER TWELVE

The next morning, Penelope tried calling Jane on the phone yet again. This time when there was no answer, she knew she had to go to the authorities.

One man in particular.

It was Sunday, so she wasn't even sure if Detective Prescott would be in. The officer at the front desk was a different man from last time, and today she didn't have a boxed lunch as a guise to expedite her access to the second floor.

"I was hoping to speak to Detective Prescott about an urgent matter."

"If you have a crime to report—"

"Oh no, it's not that, it's a *very* private matter. Is he in today?"

The officer scrutinized her. "You know it's a Sunday, right?"

"Does that mean the police department closes for the day? How fortuitous for the criminals of New York," she said with a teasing smile.

He was not amused.

"Detective Prescott is not scheduled to be in today."

"Oh," Penelope said, deflating. "I suppose he'll be here tomorrow?"

"He will. Will your *very private* matter keep til then?"

Penelope pursed her lips but wasn't without some amusement at his impertinence. She probably deserved it. Still, it seemed her favorite detective wasn't there. She was just about to leave when Detective Prescott appeared, walking down the steps from the second floor.

"I thought I heard the sound of trouble." There was a hint of a smile in his eyes and around the edges of his mouth. "Have you been harassing one of our officers?"

Penelope decided to be just as playful with him. "I wasn't harassing him I was simply inquiring. When did that become a crime?"

Detective Prescott studied her the way a parent would a disruptive child. "Did you find your anonymous body?"

"No, that's what I've come to you about. I'm concerned that I may have another."

"Two bodies in less than a week?" His brow cinched together in consternation.

The officer next to her sat up straighter with alerted interest, giving Penelope a harder look.

"Not bodies, names. Also, I don't know for a fact that they're dead, just missing."

Detective Prescott exhaled, briefly closing his eyes. "You'd better come upstairs."

Penelope smiled, then turned to raise an eyebrow at the officer before she followed Detective Prescott back upstairs. The officer stared back as though she really was trouble.

On the second floor, she noted that it was much quieter but Detective Prescott was hardly the only one getting in a day of work this weekend.

Back at his desk, she took the chair next to him as before. "If I'd known for sure that you were in today, I would have brought lunch again."

"I try to avoid dancing too close to the line of bribery. I'm just here to make headway on a few cases. But I suppose I could always add more work to my pile. So tell me about this *potentially* missing person."

"There's a bit more to it. I should probably tell you so you have the proper context."

Penelope told him about everything that seemed directly related to Jane up to and including the fact that she hadn't answered the phone this morning.

"This Mr. Pulley, you said you had lunch with him? Just the two of you?"

A smile spread her lips. "Don't tell me you're jealous?"

"Not at all," he replied, clearing his throat. "I'm just concerned you're being too reckless about this. To be frank, Miss Banks—"

"Penelope."

"—Miss Banks, this string of burglaries should be left to the police to investigate."

"I'm only looking into it as a result of my missing husband case, which the police seemed to have washed their hands of, thank you very much. But now there's Jane who's missing as well."

"You do have a point. I'll officially file a missing person's case, but it has to be handled by the precinct for the Upper West Side, mind you. I'll have the photo of the couple delivered to them."

"Thank you," Penelope said gratefully.

"I'm almost afraid to ask, but are there any other missing persons?"

"No, but there is a missing cat I'm also looking into."

"A missing cat?" He seemed to be holding back a smile.

"Lady. The burglar took her as well, in case the police are interested in investigating."

"Did he?" Now the smile was evident.

"You presume it's a he?" Penelope retorted smartly.

"And you presume a burglar, male or female, would decide to take a cat while they are snatching valuables?"

"Well, no," she said, lowering her eyelids and offering a pert smile. "But I do want to find her, if only for her own welfare. Just look at the dreary weather outside. It might start snowing at any moment. Also, this burglar, *male* or *female*, seems to be a thief of information, not just valuable goods. They found out who Daisy was being, ahem, *maintained* by."

"Hardly a crime."

"It is if they're blackmailing him—or perhaps worse."

"Don't tell me this is a third missing-or-dead person?" His brow creased.

"No, he's still alive." She stopped to consider that. "At least I think so."

"I find it very disturbing that you have a continuously growing list of people whose status as 'still breathing' is in dispute."

"Before you start getting ideas, I'm certainly not responsible for ridding them of their breath." She stopped to consider that again. "At least I hope not."

"Penelope Banks, you truly are a remarkable woman."

There was no indication that Pen should have interpreted that as a compliment. Still, she was rather tickled by it.

"Are we finally using first names now?"

Detective Richard Prescott's mouth turned down on the sides. "Tell me more about this benefactor of Daisy's."

"He's obviously someone wealthy, which means he's probably important. I suspect he must live on the Upper West Side, otherwise, why would he set Daisy up in an apartment so far from the Silver Palace where she—"

"What do you know about the Silver Palace?" Detective Prescott interrupted, his brow furrowing.

"What do *you* know about it?" Pen asked, pretending to be scandalized.

"I know that it isn't the sort of place a young lady on her own should go."

Penelope laughed. "Well, not to worry detective, my purity, reputation, and personal welfare were firmly protected. I took Benny, Benjamin Davenport. You remember him from Long Island."

Detective Prescott frowned as though that wasn't very reassuring.

"It *is* quite the show though, isn't it?" she inquired, wondering if he had seen it.

"Not for long. If certain factions had their way, it would already be closed for business. Not exactly the most wholesome image for New York."

"Since when has New York ever been wholesome?" Penelope scoffed with a laugh.

That at least earned her a begrudging smile.

"At any rate, her benefactor's name is Jameson, probably with a last name that starts with D. Spanky called him JD." Penelope wrinkled her brow as she looked off to the side in thought. "I know a few Jamesons who are wealthy, but I'm not quite as familiar with people on the West Side—new money—not that there's anything wrong with that. Heaven knows I'm probably new money myself in a way, so who am I to—

"Charlotte's hat!" Detective Prescott said aloud.

Penelope blinked once then laughed. "Did you just say 'Charlotte's hat?' And you laugh at me for my 'pineapples.'"

"Never mind that," he said grimacing.

"Do you know which Jameson I'm talking about?" Pen asked animatedly.

"Stop. Talking. Are you trying to get both of us in trouble?" he hissed.

Penelope flinched, then leaned in with an excited whisper. "You *do* know him! He must be some kind of muckety muck for him to cause this much of a stir. Who is he?"

Detective Prescott looked around then stood up, taking Penelope by the hand—which she didn't mind one little bit—and leading her away. He escorted her to what looked like an interrogation room and closed the door.

"You're sure she said Jameson?"

"Yes," Penelope said, feeling slightly impatient now. "Who is he?"

Detective Prescott studied her. "I'm not sure I should tell you."

"Would you rather I go around asking publicly?"

His jaw hardened. Even with the way it pulled at his scar, or maybe because of it, it made him look that much more handsome. "Aren't you supposed to be discreet in your business?"

"I'm *supposed* to get information in my business," Penelope pointed out. "If this Jameson has already been blackmailed, he probably knows who the burglar is. Which means he also may know who is responsible for Frank's disappearance."

"Which makes it a police matter."

"And will the police even bother spending resources to find out what happened to Frank, or Daisy's missing cat for that matter? No, they won't. Which makes it a Penelope Banks matter."

He sighed in exasperation. "This is exactly what I was worried about when you went into business."

"I remember you expressing as much," she said tartly.

He breathed out a laugh, which made her concede a laugh as well.

"Oh come now, do you really want me out there meddling on my own?"

He observed her for a moment then spoke. "Jameson Dixon Martin."

"Jameson Martin?" Penelope knew that name well enough. He was a recent addition to the wealthy class, having cleverly invested in a franchise of filling stations at which cars could refuel. She'd never learned his middle name. She had assumed the D in JD was for a last name.

"Why are you so worried about him? I mean, yes he has money but—"

"He's also *extremely* close to the police commissioner. I'd be willing to bet that's why the Silver Palace is still up and running if this Daisy Fairchild is a performer there."

"Not for long..." Penelope said slowly, putting that piece of information together with the rest. "Daisy is moving on to *Ziegfeld Follies*. With her gone, there's no longer a reason for Jameson to offer the Silver Palace protection."

This news certainly made the fate of Spanky and all the other girls from the Silver Palace seem far more dire than they'd indicated at Daisy's party. But Spanky had mentioned something about having a plan for "resurrection."

"That look on your face doesn't make me think you're going to quit working on this case."

Penelope blinked and turned her attention to Detective Prescott. "Would it make you feel better if I said I was only going to work on finding Daisy's missing cat?"

"No."

She laughed.

"This is hardly a laughing matter."

"In which case, you'd better get the force working on this case promptly. I'd hate to upstage them by solving it before they do." Penelope rose, eager to get back to work. She had an idea of where to get more information.

"Where are you going?"

"You're not the only one catching up on work on a Sunday."

"Miss Banks, you aren't going to do something dangerous are you?"

"That depends."

"On what?" His brows came together with a concerned look.

"Do you know how to pick a lock?"

"*What?*"

"It's not for anything illegal."

"Really?" he asked in an exasperated voice.

"Okay, maybe a tiny bit, but it's for the greater good."

"I feel like I should arrest you preemptively, if only for *your* own good."

"We both know how it works out when you try to detain me."

"Me having to come to your rescue yet again? That reminder only proves that this time I need a lock and key to hold you. Perhaps a jail cell."

"I'll take that as my cue to leave," she said brightly. "I'll be sure to give you some of the credit when I solve the case, *Richard*."

She hurried out of the room before he could protest any further, or worse follow through on his threat. She wouldn't put it past Detective Prescott to actually put her in jail for her own good.

At any rate, she suddenly had at least a few more people with motives for needing dough and who had access to Winchester Court Apartments. And she knew exactly where to get more information about them.

CHAPTER THIRTEEN

"The Silver Palace? Don't tell me you're changing careers already, Pen. I thought you were drowning in kale?"

"It's not for me, it's for my latest case. I finally have an interesting one, though it may be far more complicated than I thought."

Penelope was at the Peacock Club in Harlem, formerly one of her most lucrative locations at which to play cards. It was a jazz club that was laxer than other places, like the segregated Cotton Club, when it came to the races intermingling. For many people, that bit of risqué was the appeal—that and the abundance of contraband alcohol served.

For Penelope, it meant comfortably having a drink with Lucille "Lulu" Simmons. Lulu was the one who had once helped her navigate the more unsavory underworld of gambling and illegally obtained "medicinal" brandy.

"My, my, my, this detecting business is much more interesting than I thought," Lulu hummed with a smile, her stunning, cat-like eyes studying Penelope with amusement.

"You're welcome to change careers yourself and join

me," Pen offered, somewhat hoping her old friend would accept. She was beginning to realize that being able to talk things out with a second person was a benefit in this job, and Lulu was one of the savviest people she knew.

Lulu laughed and lifted her glass. "I think I'll settle for the champagne. I can't imagine what my mama would think, me chasing down criminals. She already assumes I'm bad news, singing jazz at night. "

"Does she know where you are right now?" Pen asked with a smirk.

"She knows I'm out with a friend, and that's all she's gonna know," Lulu replied smartly. "Now that I know you're looking into the Silver Palace, I'm sure she'd have a heart attack if I joined you. Not that *she* knows what goes on there, mind you."

"So you know of it?"

"I've *heard* of it," she said, making it quite clear she had nothing to do with the place.

Pen grinned. "So what have you *heard*?"

Lucille took a sip of her champagne and eyed Pen over the rim. After pulling it away and swallowing she took a breath and exhaled. "I'm not one to talk dirty about any fellow performers but I do know girls only end up working there for one of two reasons. Either their only talent lies in what they look like, and I mean below the neck if you get my drift. Or, they have a history that keeps them from working at more legitimate venues."

Penelope thought about the show she'd seen. It was true that most of the ladies on stage were lovely, though somewhat lacking in the talent department. Even Daphne, as pretty as she was, could have used a few singing lessons if she wanted to replace Daisy. But Daisy had a nice enough voice and could dance. So what was her sordid history?

"Does that go for the producers and others involved with creating the show?"

"*Especially* them," Lulu said with a laugh. She raised an eyebrow and tilted her head toward the club behind her. "But that's true of most places."

Penelope chose to sip her drink rather than comment. The Peacock Club definitely had its ties to the criminal world.

"Now you've got me curious, what *is* this case you're working on? I don't need names, just a taste."

It probably couldn't hurt to tell Lulu some of it, if only to get her input. After all, Pen had already told Cousin Cordelia and Benny most of it.

"I have a woman whose husband is missing. He was supposed to be traveling for business but he didn't end up where he was supposed to be. It's now been almost a week since he was due to return."

"So either dead or he left her, and she hired you for that?" Lulu looked skeptical.

"I suppose she'd like to know which of those it is," Penelope said. "Also, where was he if he wasn't where he said he was going to be?"

"How does she know that?"

Penelope hesitated, then told her about the bus accident.

"All the passengers have been accounted for. It took me long enough to finally get through to the company that owns the line. The vultures from the press are probably *still* circling that tragedy." Penelope felt her ire grow. With Agnes's murder, she'd seen firsthand the depths to which certain sleazy actors would sink when it came to death and tragedy.

"They really do have no shame," Lucille agreed. "Do

you know one of them once offered me five dollars for a firsthand account of when Liam 'The Diamond' McBride got shot at Frankie's down the way?"

"Five dollars?"

"Indeed," Lucille said with a sly smile. "I asked for ten, then lied through my teeth."

Penelope erupted with laughter.

"That included giving him a fake name, mind you. I don't need every other so-and-so coming after me by being stupid enough to get my name in the papers."

A smart thing, especially about such a scandalous topic.

"Here's an idea, maybe he *was* on that bus and he's been claimed by someone who knew him by another name. I knew a woman who found out her man had a whole other family in a different state. Lord save me, it's bad enough just thinking about one marriage, why would anyone want two?"

Penelope smiled. This was the kind of creative thinking she needed for a case like this.

"A bigamist?" Pen sipped and mulled that one over. It made some sense, but that would have meant Frank's second family missed him three weeks of the month when he was with Jane. That was a long time to be gone, even if you despised your husband.

Still, it might explain why he didn't like having his photo taken. It might also explain him getting married *supposedly* for the first time at such a late age in life, especially to someone as guileless as Jane.

"That would be expensive. Though, he has money, if her apartment and clothes are any indication."

"Oh?" Lulu said, her eyes brightening at the mention of clothes. She designed her own and always looked spectacular because of it. Right now she wore a champagne silk dress with layered scalloped-edged skirts that fell high enough to show off long, brown legs that were the very definition of gams.

That was another fun thing about going out that Pen liked, dressing up. She was in a two-tone dress with a dark coral, sleeveless top underneath a black lace overdress, and a large black bow at the waist. Her layered black lace skirts fell just below the knees with an uneven hemline.

Penelope described Jane's coat and dress for Lulu.

"Hmm, definitely well made. If he has two families, he's getting money from somewhere. What does he do?"

"He travels, selling Bibles with a custom gold imprint of the family name on the covers."

Lulu laughed out loud. "Pen, heaven knows my mama forces me to go to church often enough, heathen that I am. And those pews are packed every Sunday. But I seriously doubt he's making *that* much money selling Bibles. Church folk know better. If anything, any extra money is given as tithes."

Penelope had suspected as much herself, but it was nice to have those suspicions confirmed. Before she could discuss it further, they were joined by a third party.

Tommy Callahan, a handsome yet notorious green-eyed devil, sported a teasing grin as he pulled up an empty chair and sat down to join them.

"Well, well, well, if it isn't my favorite card hustler and the prettiest songbird this side of a hundred and tenth."

"I haven't come to play cards, so you can tell Mr. Sweeney to keep his distance," Penelope said, glaring at him. Tommy was the favorite henchman of the notorious gangster Jack Sweeney. Just before earning her inheritance, she had gotten into a bit of trouble playing cards with the wrong man.

"Yes, we all heard about your lucky break," he said with

a wink. "If you ever feel like investing some of that five million dollars in a profitable endeavor, be sure to let me know."

"I'll keep that in mind," she responded dryly. She wasn't surprised he knew the exact amount she had been left by Agnes.

"So what are you two ladies chatting about tonight?"

"We were discussing the disappearance of a man," she said, giving him a pointed look.

Tommy, never one to get rattled or easily offended, simply laughed in that low, slightly dangerous way of his. "Men only disappear when they have a reason to get lost. In the company of two lovely dames, why would I ever leave?"

He sat back and lit a cigarette, getting comfortable despite Pen's hint for him to leave. "Is this about a case of yours?"

Penelope sat up straighter in surprise, though in retrospect, it didn't surprise her that he also knew this much about her. The various crime families in New York probably knew more about the city's residents than anyone, especially the wealthy or notorious ones. Penelope probably fell under both headings.

"Let me tell you something, Pen, men breeze for one of three reasons, their past, present, or future," Tommy continued.

"Well, that just about covers it," Lulu said with a sardonic smile.

Tommy chuckled, casting a quick wink her way before returning his attention to Pen. He leaned in and counted on his fingers as he spoke. "One, they don't like their present. Two, they see something better for them in the future. Three, their past has caught up with them."

That was exactly what Detective Prescott had

suggested. It was funny how men, no matter where they fell on the spectrum of respectability, seemed to think alike.

One thing was certain, Frank Peterson was hiding something. Tomorrow, Penelope planned on finding out what that was when she went to visit Jane at her apartment.

She eyed the two people sitting across from her. "Do either of you know how to pick a lock?"

Lulu blinked in surprise.

Tommy laughed.

"How much is it worth to you?" he asked.

"*I'll* teach you for the cost of this drink," Lulu said, twisting her lips at him.

"Sounds to me like you might be getting yourself in a bit of trouble, Lady Pen," Tommy said. "I can sell you a gun if you need it."

Penelope rolled her eyes. "The case hasn't gotten quite *that* precarious yet."

"New York is a dangerous city and a girl who goes sticking her nose into other people's business may eventually find herself in a situation where she needs protection."

"That sounds like a threat, Tommy."

"Just a word of warning. As usual, you know where to find me if you change your mind." He gave Lulu a wry smile. "I'll leave it to you to handle the lock-picking lessons, sweetheart. Who knew you had such agile hands to go along with that voice of yours?"

"It's always a bad idea to make assumptions about a girl. Stick around and you'll find out what else I can do with these hands."

As much as Pen could have done without the company of Tommy Callahan, she would never have been that cavalier with him. Lulu certainly liked to live dangerously. Perhaps spending so much time around the criminal element gave her some immunity. Plus, she was one of the main draws to the Peacock Club.

Tommy simply laughed again before rising. He gave them a sardonic bow before sauntering away, cool and easy.

The two of them watched him leave, both breathing a bit easier.

"He does have a point, Pen. You should have some kind of weapon on you."

"Do you carry a gun?"

"Of course," Lulu said, then smiled. "A real pretty ivory-handled one."

"It's a weapon, not a fashion accessory."

"Who says it can't be both?"

Penelope finished her drink. "How about those lock-picking lessons instead? Tomorrow, I plan on sticking my nose into other people's business."

CHAPTER FOURTEEN

The next day, Penelope headed back to Winchester Court to see if Jane had finally come back. She also wanted to try out her new lock-picking skills to find out what was behind that door marked "Maintenance Only."

The cold weather had finally succumbed to snow, though it was only a flake or two that floated through the air around her at this point. They melted as soon as they hit the ground. Still, the nearly white sky didn't bode well. The only question was how much snow they would eventually get.

Pen wrapped her scarf more firmly around her neck.

She saw Mrs. Middleberry through the second-floor window as she arrived. Pen flashed a smile up as she rang for Jane's apartment. Her neighbor's voice answered instead.

"Jane hasn't returned yet. Is she no longer at her aunt's home? I certainly hope she didn't take a turn for the worse."

Fortunately, Mrs. Middleberry couldn't see Penelope's expression. It was a bit tactless to air her neighbor's business

—never mind how much of a lie it was—such that anyone walking by on the street could hear.

Still, this meant Jane hadn't come back yet. Penelope was officially worried that she may have suffered the same fate as her husband, who she assumed at this point must be dead.

But what had her hurrying out of the apartment in the first place over two days ago? What had she discovered, and why hadn't she at least called to tell Penelope what she had learned?

As much as she was determined to find out what happened to Jane, she was here now and decided to follow through on her second agenda of the day, getting past that locked door.

"I was wondering if I could ask you a favor, Mrs. Middleberry. I'd rather not discuss it on the street."

"Me?" She sounded perfectly delighted at the prospect. "Yes, yes, come up. My husband is just on his way down. He's going in late because of the weather. He's allowed to make his hours, you see."

Said husband was just opening the door as his wife informed the world that he was going in to work late. Penelope noted that it was well past ten o'clock. By the time he made it down to East 35th Street, it would be past eleven.

He didn't seem all that pleased at his wife's indiscretion, offering Penelope a tight smile as he held the door open for her.

"It looks like it's already started snowing," he offered by way of explanation.

Penelope looked out and up toward the sky. The tiny sprinkling of snowflakes seemed hardly worth going in late for. Most people would have left earlier rather than later to get into their offices ahead of worsening weather.

Even Mr. Middleberry seemed embarrassed at using such a sorry excuse for going in so late to work. He averted his gaze as Penelope passed by to enter. He hurriedly left, the door slamming shut behind him.

It occurred to Pen that she hadn't cleared him as a suspect. While she had her sights on Daisy's acquaintances after everything she'd learned about the Silver Palace this weekend, it could still just as easily be a resident. In fact, it was much easier to assume such a thing. After all, Mr. Middleberry not only had continuous, inconspicuous access, he knew his wife's schedule so he could pretend the Middleberrys had been robbed along with everyone else.

And conveniently enough the items that weren't in Mrs. Middleberry's safe were the only items taken—which all belonged to Mr. Middleberry.

That was enough to convince Penelope she should detour from trying to pick the lock and instead follow Mr. Middleberry. After all, whatever was behind that door would surely keep for a while. At least she hoped so.

"Miss Banks? Are you down there?" she heard Mrs. Middleberry call down. Her voice was enough to hurry Pen back out the door.

"Sorry, I forgot something!" Pen called out, just so she wouldn't be too upset with her.

Penelope looked down the street and saw Mr. Middleberry just about to reach the corner. He certainly didn't look like a man in a hurry to get to work.

So where was he headed?

Penelope rushed down the sidewalk to follow him, making sure to keep enough distance so that she wouldn't be seen. Today she had at least thought to wear warm and comfortable footwear.

He eventually took the Westside subway line going

south and transferred at 42nd Street to catch the Eastside line. Penelope followed him the entire way, wondering if this trip would be worth it. At this point, she wouldn't make it back up to Winchester Court until this afternoon. Thus far, it seemed he was headed exactly where he told his wife he'd be.

He got off at 33rd Street and headed north to 35th Street. Penelope sighed as she tailed him. She supposed this was all part of being a private investigator, a lot of following people, which sometimes led nowhere. She wondered which of the office buildings was his.

The snow was coming in heavier now, the fat flakes sticking to the ground. It was not quite a snowstorm yet and Penelope smiled at how pretty it made everything.

Mr. Middleberry slowed as he approached a building and Penelope studied it. Her brow wrinkled in confusion. It certainly didn't look like the type of building a Savings & Loan would be housed in, even a "special branch." It looked more like—

"Zounds!"

He was entering an apartment building!

Penelope hurried along, her brow even more creased. Mr. Middleberry certainly didn't seem like the cheating type. He was so...*ordinary*. Older, slightly balding, starting to show in the middle where all his wife's pot pies went. He didn't even dress all that impressively.

But he was still a man, after all.

Still, it wouldn't hurt to make sure an affair was all this was. He could very well be meeting his fellow thieves to divvy up any loot they'd stolen. The idea of Mr. Middleberry being involved in a complex ring of thieves seemed absurd, enough to make Penelope giggle, but that didn't mean it was impossible.

It was only as the door was closing after him that she realized the only way to make certain was to catch it before it closed. That meant exposing herself. She took two seconds to decide it was worth it and quickly caught it.

Mr. Middleberry was standing by the elevator waiting to go up. He turned with idle curiosity to see who had come in after him. When he saw Penelope, his eyes went wide, showing the whites that suddenly matched the color of his ashen face.

"You! What are you doing here?" he exclaimed, looking as guilty as anything.

CHAPTER FIFTEEN

"This certainly doesn't look like the offices for a Savings & Loan," Penelope accused, narrowing her gaze at Mr. Middleberry.

His face went from ghostly white to red with embarrassment, and he swallowed hard. "Did Ida send you?"

"No, your *wife* is still at home, blissfully unaware of what you're up to," she said in a reproachful voice.

He blinked in surprise as though Penelope had slapped him in the face.

Good, she thought. She didn't much care for Mrs. Middleberry, but no woman deserved to be cheated on, and in such a devious manner. Was he paying the rent on this apartment for his mistress? Granted, it was no Winchester Court, but still.

"It's not what you think."

Penelope laughed. She couldn't help it, the comment was so predictable.

"No, really, I'm not cheating on my wife, Miss Banks."

"Your office *just happens* to be in an apartment building?"

He opened his mouth to say something, then seemed to deflate, exhaling with dismay.

"I know this looks bad, but...why don't you come up and you'll see."

Penelope coughed out a laugh. "I'm not naïve Mr. Middleberry. I'm also not interested in whatever you are involved with up there."

"But...what are you going to tell Ida? She can't possibly think that I'm cheating on her!"

"Lucky for you she doesn't. In fact, she's probably just started baking the pot pies you love so much. Perhaps you should think about that while you're with whoever is up there!" she said, waving her hand toward the elevator.

"I already told you it isn't what you think!" he pleaded, nearly in tears. "Please just...let me show you."

He seemed agonized over this, enough to make Penelope think maybe this *wasn't* what she assumed.

"Okay, but...we're taking the stairs, and you go first. Don't you try anything, Mr. Middleberry," she warned. Perhaps she should have taken Tommy up on his offer of a weapon. Then again, Mr. Middleberry looked as though he would shatter to pieces if she said the word "boo" right now.

He quickly skittered toward the stairway, making sure to give Penelope a wide berth. She followed more slowly, leaving at least a few steps between them. He went up to the third floor and down the hallway to a door at the end. Nearly dropping his keys several times, he finally managed to open it.

"Here you are," he said, waving a hand for her to enter.

"I don't think so. You first."

He nodded with understanding and shuffled inside ahead of her. She craned her neck to peer in, mostly out of curiosity before she stepped inside. What she saw didn't impress her much. If this was where he held secret trysts it wasn't very romantic.

Penelope slowly stepped inside to get a better look, making sure to remain near the door, which she deliberately left open.

The overall color scheme seemed to be brown. There was an overstuffed sofa and several old bookcases which held a mix of paperbacks and hardbacks. On the wall were paintings of ducks and wooded landscapes. The air smelled of spicy tobacco. There was a victrola and a case with some records against a wall. To the side was a decanter that held something amber. That appeared to be the lone bit of evidence of illicit activity.

"What is this place?" Penelope asked.

"My...escape you might call it."

"Escape?" she repeated, turning to him in confusion.

"I love my wife, Miss Banks, I really do. But, I simply need a place where I can escape, do the things I enjoy doing like reading a book in peace and quiet or smoking a cigar, which she expressly forbids my doing in the apartment. Sometimes just relaxing and listening to music."

"What happened to your job?"

"I did quit my old job. Frankly, I hated it all twenty-five years I worked there. Day in and day out, that lifeless, mind-numbing, routine wore on me. I was happy to quit, *more* than happy. I thought I could be happy at home with Ida but, after a month I realized my folly. A husband and wife just aren't meant to spend that much time together."

Penelope thought that was a definite statement about his marriage rather than the institution itself, but what did she know? Each marriage was different.

"I couldn't go back to that job. I just couldn't. At first,

I'd take my little excursions outside for a few hours, but she always wanted to come with me. I couldn't tell her I needed time to myself, her feelings get hurt so easily, you know. So... I thought of this." He waved his hand around. "I made up the job just so she wouldn't get suspicious or upset."

"Aren't you worried she'll find out? What if she wants to visit you at the office?"

"In twenty-five years of marriage, she has come to visit me at the office less than five times, and then only when invited or due to an emergency. I figured this would be the same. The first month, I leased a shared office space just in case. I let it lapse when I realized she was fine at home knowing I was supposedly away at work."

"And the money your aunt left you pays for all of this? *Two* apartment rentals in New York?"

He breathed out a weary laugh. "Aunt Deborah may have been the black sheep of the Middleberry family, but she did have a talent for picking very wealthy husbands and then outliving them. I was the nephew who outlived *her*. I never made any fuss about her life. I think she appreciated that. Live and let live, I say. It worked out for me."

"So you just stay here all day?"

"When the weather is not so nice, as it is now. Otherwise, I explore, go to museums, walk through the park, maybe take in a picture show occasionally. The library is a favorite of mine, that's why I rented a place within walking distance."

That didn't sound like such a terrible way to pass the day.

Still, that didn't mean she'd take him at his word.

"But you started coming home for lunch in the past month. Why is that?" The burglaries had only begun during the same time period.

He seemed confused by the question but answered. "One thing I can say about Ida is that she's a very good cook. Also, sometimes I do miss her during the long hours I'm supposed to be at work. When the weather is nice, I prefer to buy something boxed and maybe sit at the park and eat, watch people go by. It's surprisingly peaceful, even here in the city. In winter, well, it's different obviously. I made up a story about being able to take long lunches."

Penelope twisted her lips in thought. Having met Mrs. Middleberry, she could perfectly understand only being able to tolerate her in small doses. And if a man had inherited a nice sum and hated his job, why not quit? This apartment, which probably made him feel like a bachelor again, was a very nice compromise.

And made him less of a suspect.

"I suppose that makes sense," Penelope said with a resigned sigh.

"You won't tell her, will you? You can make up something when you report back to her. Just say I really am working at an office."

"I don't plan on telling your wife anything, Mr. Middleberry. That's for you to do."

"But, won't she wonder? Isn't that why you're here? She hired you, right? To follow me?"

Penelope gave him a confused smile. "No, I...to be honest, I'm looking into these burglaries."

He exhaled and sank to the couch with relief. "Thank goodness. So Ida doesn't suspect a thing?"

"No, but she is thrilled to have you home for lunch. You might think about occasionally going back even when the weather is nicer."

"So...wait a second, you didn't suspect me of the burglaries, did you?" He coughed out a laugh.

"How is that so funny? You're right there where it happens, and you do live a duplicitous existence."

"That's fair, I suppose," he nodded, then breathed out a small laugh. "The funny thing is, this is just the sort of thing I'd tell Ida about. Me being considered a suspect in a crime. She'd have a laugh over it as well."

"I think perhaps it is wise to keep this to yourself. But be sure to have a much more judicious explanation handy if she finds out. No woman likes to feel as though their presence is unwanted, even if it makes sense."

He nodded with understanding.

"So, you're looking into these burglaries? For my wife's sake, I do hope you find the guy. Honestly, for my sake too. She's talking about moving, and I just can't go through that again. I let her do that place up exactly the way she wanted. She wants to live like Marie Antoinette, who am I to complain? *Vive la France*, I say. That's where we went on our honeymoon. I even paid for a decorator to do the whole thing so it didn't look like a complete disaster. Thank God we gave the place in Yonkers to Thomas and his wife, otherwise she would have already had us moving back. I prefer the city. Especially now." He looked around as though this explained his desire to stay. "But isn't that for the police to worry about?"

"It's more complicated than that."

"Is this about the Petersons?"

Penelope didn't respond, but he guessed as much. "Strange couple, and not just because they spend so much time together." His brow rose as though that defied explanation. "Though, he's another one who's probably living a double life."

"What? How do you know?"

He was silent, the look on his face indicating he wished he hadn't said anything.

"Would you prefer I go back and tell Ida about your *bachelor* apartment?" She didn't like blackmailing him this way, and she certainly had no intention of telling Ida about this, but he didn't know that.

He frowned and then sighed. "I shouldn't have said that. For all I know, maybe he does sell those Bibles of his for a living. Perhaps he's the religious type and it's a calling or something. But I can tell you one thing, Miss Banks, that certainly isn't where his money is coming from."

"What do you mean?" Pen asked, curious as to what his explanation would be.

He gave her a dry smile. "I work in finance, Miss Banks —or at least I did. There's no money in selling Bibles door to door, I don't care how fancy you make them. Not enough to live on the Upper West Side. Who knows, maybe he had his own Aunt Eleanor to leave him something?"

Or perhaps something more sinister.

Suddenly, Penelope really needed to find out where Jane might be. This detour had turned out to be somewhat fruitful in a concerning way.

"Thank you Mr. Middleberry," she said, turning to go.

"You won't tell, Ida, right?" he called out.

"Your secret is safe with me," she called back.

She decided to take a taxi back to the apartment building rather than the subway. Even then, with New York traffic, it was early afternoon by the time she got back.

Penelope called up for Jane, and was not surprised when there was no answer. Still, it made her heart sink. At this point, perhaps Detective Prescott had a point, she did need to leave it to the authorities. Jane was definitely in trouble. It was time to go to the police department that handled this part of the city and lay a little pressure on them.

"Are you Penelope Banks?"

She turned in surprise at the sound of her name. The man she saw didn't look like the friendly sort, and not just because he wasn't smiling. He studied her with hard eyes, as though she had personally done him wrong.

"Who wants to know?"

Wrong answer.

The next thing she knew, he had a gun secretly pointed at her and an even more menacing look on his face.

"I do, and you're coming with me, lady."

CHAPTER SIXTEEN

Penelope had never had a gun pointed at her before. She became paralyzed with fear. That lasted about five seconds before she considered screaming. It was still the lunch hour and there were people around, surely one of them would come to her aid?

"Don't even think about it, sweetheart."

She looked up at the windows above but was dismayed to see that neither Mrs. Middleberry nor Adam Pulley happened to be looking out right now. Of all the times!

"Where's my money?"

That surprised her. "What money?"

His jaw hardened. "I'm going to ask one more time before I get nasty about it. Where is—"

"I don't know what money you're talking about!" she said, raising her voice in the hopes that someone would hear and come to her rescue.

"I can see you're going to be difficult about this."

The man reached out to grab her arm and pull her closer. At first, her mind went to the absolute worst-case scenario. Then, she remembered he had asked for her by name. This wasn't a random attack. He pressed the end of the gun into her side, and she realized he was using her as cover to hide it while he practically dragged her away.

"You wouldn't dare shoot me, not with all these people around."

"I have six bullets that say otherwise. And you have no idea what I'm capable of, lady. You think you'd be the first person I ever shot? The last one was a dame too, in case you're mistaking me for the type of man that has morals."

"You shot a woman?"

He laughed, low and sardonically. "You dames, you want the vote but suddenly get all outraged when it comes to equality everywhere else."

"I didn't mean it that way, I meant—"

"Just shut up and get into the car," he said, opening the passenger side of a car parked on the street.

For some idiotic reason, she wanted to continue protesting that she hadn't meant to focus on the woman part of what he'd said so much as the shooting part. But that thought vanished when she realized he was forcing her into a car that was already running. Which meant a ride somewhere. Probably far away.

"No."

He stared at her in disbelief, his eyes so wide it would have been comical under any other circumstance.

"Need I remind you about the gun?"

"You'll get caught."

"And I'll go down shooting, starting with you. I'm a desperate man, Miss Banks. Desperation makes a man do crazy things, like shoot a dame in broad daylight."

Rather than wait for a response, he shoved her inside and followed, forcing her in even more. He shut the door behind them.

That's when she did scream. It was instantly silenced when he stabbed her in the side with the gun. Even through her winter coat, it hurt.

"Ouch!"

"Shut up and drive," he said.

"I can't."

"What did I say about—"

"I mean I—I don't know how to drive."

"What?" He was incredulous.

"This is New York! Why would I learn how to drive?"

He growled and shook his head in wonder, cursing under his breath.

"Maybe if you just told me why you think I have your money, we wouldn't have to go through all of this."

"I have a better idea," he said, glaring hard. "Today is the day you're gonna learn how to drive."

"What if I hit someone?" she asked in alarm.

He leaned in closer, enough for her to see how dangerous he was. "So don't hit anyone."

He instructed her on what to do and they managed to clunk along down the street. She panicked when they hit the more crowded Amsterdam Avenue, but the gun he stuck into her side helped her quickly overcome it.

It certainly didn't help that the snow was coming in heavier. Much heavier. At least it had the benefit of keeping most drivers off the streets.

"Are you Frank's friend?"

"Frank," he muttered, then gave a short sharp laugh.

"Did you kill him?"

"He's dead?" He turned to her in surprise.

Which answered her question.

"Where'd you hear he was dead?" he pressed.

"I don't know that he is, I just thought..." She didn't want to say it out loud.

"Thought what?"

"I thought you were the one who killed him. You are the one with the gun after all."

"So is he dead or not?" he asked impatiently.

"You tell me!" she said in a shrill voice, the stress of operating the damnable car and dealing with him finally getting to her. Driving cars wasn't nearly as fun as riding in them.

"I just want what's mine, and you're the one who's going to—hey, watch out!" Penelope came to a screeching halt just in time to avoid running a red light. "Jesus, lady, you're going to get us both killed."

She turned to give him an incredulous look.

"Just keep your eyes on the road."

"Are you John Keyes?"

"Who's John Keyes?"

So that was a no.

"Is he the one who has my money?"

"Your money?"

"Don't play dumb with me, I'm in no mood."

"I don't know anything about any money, and I have no idea who John Keyes is. Why do you think I asked you?"

"Don't get smart either. I was told you knew where Frank was, and if not that, where my money was."

"I don't!"

"We'll see about that."

"What does that mean?"

"You'll see. Shut up and drive. No more questions."

"But—" she went quiet at the feel of his gun against her side again.

How in the world was this happening? This was

supposed to be a simple missing husband case! Maybe a missing cat case. Now she was stuck in the car with a man pointing a gun at her.

"Did you kill Jane?"

"What did I say about questions?"

"Did you?" she insisted, feeling her heart pound. She hadn't known Jane that long, but the thought of her being murdered, all because she fell in love was almost devastating.

"She's alive. For now."

The words felt as daunting as he meant them to be. Still, Penelope felt some bit of relief that she was still breathing.

She remained faithfully quiet the rest of the drive until they were practically in Inwood. He had her drive to a small house on a street that looked half deserted. She stopped the car and he did something to turn off the engine.

"Scream all you want out here, there's no one to hear you, honey." He grinned. "Now, I'm gonna get out first and then let you out. Don't try anything that might make me inadvertently pull this trigger."

Penelope searched the area with wild eyes. Dusk was rapidly approaching, which did absolutely nothing to calm her fears.

This is it, I'm going to die out here!

She took a few breaths, enough to calm herself by the time he opened the door on her side. Now the gun was visible instead of tucked into his body. Her purse was on the seat next to her, having fallen there when she was practically thrown into the car. Once again she rued not taking Tommy up on his offer for a gun. He yanked her out before she could grab the purse. Of course, it being stolen was the least of her concerns right now.

He had her walk ahead of him straight up to the small house. The door was unlocked and she went inside. The interior was surprisingly quaint and old-fashioned, making her think it belonged to his grandmother perhaps. She certainly hoped he hadn't killed the owner just to have a place to keep Penelope kidnapped.

"Keep going, this ain't no tour," he warned, leading her to a door that led to the basement. There was a single light, which left a lot of the space in shadows. Everywhere she looked there was a shovel or hammer or some other tool. It only instilled more fear in her.

It took a moment for her eyes to adjust, but there was no mistaking the figure gagged and bound to a chair.

"Jane! You're alive!" Penelope ran over and instinctively pulled the gag from her mouth.

"Hey, what the hell do you think you're doing?"

"Are you okay?" Pen asked, still focused on her client.

"I don't know! I don't know what he wants! He called and asked me to meet him. He said he knew Frank. I thought Frank was in trouble so I just left without thinking. That's when he pulled out the gun and..." Jane wailed for a moment before taking a breath to continue. "Eventually I told him I had hired someone to find Frank. I'm sorry, I told him your name, Miss Banks. I had to, I thought he was going to kill me!"

"It's okay, I'm just glad you're safe. Let's get you out of these ropes and—"

"Hey!" The man shouted, this time loudly enough to draw both their attention.

Penelope spun around, glaring at him. "This is how you go about getting information? Terrorizing innocent women?"

"I'll do a lot more than terrorize if you don't shut up and tell me where my money is."

"That's a contradiction."

His brow wrinkled in confusion, then creased in anger. "What did I say about getting smart? Now, you're gonna sit in that second chair. I don't want to have to go to the trouble of tying you up as well. Frankly, I can't be bothered. Just tell me what I want to hear and we can be done with this."

Penelope sat down and gave him a cool look. "You're going to kill us either way."

"What?" Jane cried.

He returned a half-smile, looking crueler than ever. Then he chuckled, removing his coat. Underneath, he wore a ridiculous suit in a bright blue-green color that shimmered even in this dim light. It must have involved a generous amount of silk. The stripes were broad enough for her to see that they were gold and red. He wore the jacket closed over his broad chest with shiny, decorative buttons that he probably polished each night. Combined with the two-tone shoes he looked like a perfect clown. One who liked flashy things it seemed.

"What *are* you wearing?" Penelope asked, unable to help herself.

He gave her a haughty look that only made him seem more hilarious. "This suit cost me five hundred dollars."

"Gracious me," muttered Jane.

Penelope grimaced. Some men were too vain for their own good. Perhaps whoever took his money was trying to do him a favor fashion-wise.

"Now, once again, where is my money? I know Frank had it. It's been almost two weeks now. He hasn't paid up like he was supposed to."

"I already told you, Frank sells Bibles. You have the

wrong man. Just let us go, we promise not to tell," Jane pleaded.

Penelope wasn't nearly so naïve, especially after speaking with Mr. Middleberry. "It would help if you gave us the details. Why is it you think that Frank Peterson owes you money?"

"Now, why would I tell you that? You looking for me to incriminate myself?"

"Beyond kidnapping, you mean?" She gave him a pointed look.

He seemed to consider that and shook his head. "No, I don't think so."

She exhaled in exasperation. "We both know you're going to kill us, so why not tell us everything? Confession is good for the soul."

"Miss Banks!" Jane was almost hysterical.

Penelope ignored Jane, realizing that it was pointless trying to reassure her. Their best chance of staying alive was persuading this man to keep them alive. He seemed to be considering what she was saying, but she was disappointed to see him shake his head yet again.

"Tell me who this John Keyes is."

"Him again?" Jane asked, looking back and forth between the two of them and settling on Pen. "What does he have to do with this?"

"I asked if he was John Keyes, or maybe it's John Key. Mrs. Middleberry claimed she heard your husband say he was going to try and keep in touch with him."

Jane stared at her in confusion, but gradual realization began to reflect on her face. "Do you mean *jonquille*?"

Now Penelope was the confused one—until realization slowly dawned on her as well.

"*Jonquille*?" she repeated with a laugh. "I can't believe I didn't figure that out."

"Well, the way Mrs. Middleberry probably pronounced it, it's no wonder. Frank calls me that every time he leaves."

"Someone want to tell me what the hell a daffodil has to do with anything?"

Penelope turned to him in surprise, realizing he had perfectly translated the word. "You speak French?"

For some reason, this seemed to upset him. "Never you mind what I do and don't speak. You've got bigger problems, like what's going to happen to you if I don't get my money. Because right now, neither of you seems to know, which makes you both expendable."

Having wasted so much time focused on John Key-or-Keyes, Penelope dismissed it in favor of giving this man something useful, or at least something that might keep them alive a while longer.

While Jane cried and pled their case, Penelope quickly worked her brain, pouring over everything she learned about Frank Peterson, which was infuriatingly little. The contents of that box of his were of little value.

"I've got it!"

The other two occupants of the basement perked up.

"What do you know?" Jane was the first to ask. "Is it about Frank?"

"Or better yet, my money?"

Penelope focused on their captor, giving him a bold look. "Both. I know exactly what you're after, and I know exactly where it is."

CHAPTER SEVENTEEN

The man with the gun leaned in and Penelope could see the gleam in his eye. "You know where my money is?"

"Better than that, something even more valuable to you."

He managed a soft laugh. "More valuable than money? This better be good."

"A silver button?" She eyed his flamboyant clothing. The man might as well have been a peacock. "It is yours isn't it?"

The color seemed to drain from his face, and Penelope knew her stab in the dark was accurate. He rushed over, causing her to flinch in surprise.

"What do you know about that button?"

Pen swallowed, then quickly pulled herself together.

"Do you really need me to explain it to you?" She scoffed, even exhaling a small sardonic laugh to maintain the facade that hid her complete and utter ignorance. She had no idea what the significance of that button was. "After all, there's a reason Frank held onto it all this time."

"And you have it?"

This confirmed a sneaking, yet disappointing suspicion she had. He had no idea where the button was, which meant he wasn't the thief who'd stolen the things from Frank's box—or the apartments of everyone else who'd been robbed at Winchester Court.

Still, that didn't mean he hadn't killed Frank.

If Frank was indeed dead.

Good grief, she was utterly clueless.

At this point, if Frank wasn't dead, Penelope would happily do the deed herself for all the trouble he'd caused.

"It's in my purse, which I left in your car."

He narrowed his eyes, studying her hard as though trying to determine if she was lying. In the end, he seemed to come to the conclusion that it wouldn't hurt to check.

Until he realized she was still unbound. Penelope could almost see the debate in his head as to whether he should take the time to tie her up or take the risk of leading her back outside so she stayed in his sights.

She hoped it was the latter. That would at least give her a fighting chance, as reckless as it would be. Still, it was better than the certain death they faced when he realized she was lying.

"Up," he said, motioning with the gun.

Penelope slowly rose, trying not to be too obvious as she scanned the area in her periphery. She needed a tool that would help her do the dirty deed of attacking him, thus giving her a fighting chance. There were almost too many to choose from.

"Don't get any ideas," the man growled, as though reading her mind. He was right behind her, gun pointed at her back.

She nodded and made her way to the stairs, finally

deciding on what to use. When she neared the shovel, she stumbled, instinctively reaching out to catch herself. In some awkwardly acrobatic feat, she made it to the floor, grasping the shovel in her hand and rapidly spinning around with as much force as she could muster. The momentum seemed to help and the bladed side fell flush against his wrist.

A loud bang filled the air as he fired. Penelope flinched, waiting for the pain to erupt somewhere on her body. It took her a moment to realize she hadn't been hit. She saw him lift his arm to aim at her for another shot. She scrambled to try and swing the shovel back to give him another good whack but realized she wouldn't have time.

However, that didn't matter when they both saw the state of his wrist, which seemed to bend at an odd angle.

"You damn broad, you broke my wrist!"

By way of response, Pen fully swung the shovel back and hit him again, this time rising high enough to aim for the head. He remained standing, reeling on the spot for a few seconds before slumping to the ground.

"Oh! Did you kill him?" Jane cried.

"With any luck," Penelope gritted out as she scrambled to her feet.

She reached down to quickly snatch the gun away from his limp hand. When her eyes rose to meet Jane's she saw they were so wide she thought they might escape her face.

"He's not dead," she reassured her. Pen could see the slight rise and fall of his chest even though he was completely out.

She grabbed a saw, which seemed handy enough, and brought it back to work away at the rope keeping Jane bound to the chair. It took a minute and Pen's heart raced the whole time, waiting for the man to rise again. He was bigger than both of them and while she was working on Jane's binding she couldn't exactly focus on shooting him.

"Okay, I need you to hold this," she said to Jane once she was free. She handed the gun to her. "I need to try tying this guy up before he comes to."

"You want *me* to hold the gun?"

"It's either that or you do the tying?"

"Can't we just leave?"

"Do you want to find out about Frank or not?"

Jane paused, her eyelids fluttering with dismay.

"You probably won't even need to use it," Pen reassured her. "Most people are perfectly cowed just by the threat of a gun. But you will have to keep it aimed at him if he wakes up. And you may even have to pull the trigger. Just...try not to accidentally hit me."

"Oh!" she fretted.

Pen didn't waste time trying to reassure her yet again. The man wasn't dead and if he woke up, the situation would be ten times more problematic. Instead, she searched out the rope and used it to bind his hands first.

She had just made the first loop around his wrists when he came to, violently swinging his unharmed arm out and striking her hard enough across the face to send her reeling back onto her behind.

He seemed like Frankenstein, the way he flailed and groaned incoherently, but it was too late to try and wrangle him now. Pen's abilities were no match for his strength, even in a half-lucid state. She was nearest him, so he focused all his attention on her, completely missing the woman with the gun to his left.

"I'm going to kill you!"

He lunged. She heard a loud bang in the air.

"Oh my God, I killed him!"

Pen was staring right into his eyes, close enough to see the whites. The pupils they surrounded looked anything but dead; they looked enlarged with rage. A string of curses escaped his mouth as he rolled onto the floor lifting the leg that had been struck with a bullet and holding it with his uninjured hand.

"He's not dead," Penelope rasped out as she got to her feet. She rescued the gun from Jane and handed her the shovel instead. "Good job though. Perfect aim, I'd say."

He rewarded them with another string of curses in between howls of pain.

"Hey, you watch your language in front of the lady," Penelope scolded.

When he responded with even filthier language she walked over and kicked him in the shin that had been shot. He roared in pain and anger.

"Oh stop, you're the one who said no one could hear you out here." She leaned in and smiled. "Which means now you're the one who is going to give us some answers."

CHAPTER EIGHTEEN

"I'm not telling you a damn thing."

"Jane hit him in the injured leg with the shovel."

"*What?*"

Penelope could hear the horror in Jane's voice behind her, but she kept her eyes on the man lying before her. The way he flinched told her she had at least some leverage.

"I'll make her do it if you don't start talking. Tell us everything you know about Frank and your relationship with him, starting with your name."

He narrowed his eyes, but she didn't waver.

"I ain't telling you my name, but I can tell you *his* ain't Frank." A smirk came to his face as his eyes slid past Penelope to Jane. "It's Pierre. Pierre Wilson."

"Pierre?" Jane repeated, coming in closer. "Isn't that French?"

"For Peter, as in Peterson," Penelope said next to her. "But his real last name isn't French."

The man gave her a cool look, as though waiting for her to piece it together further.

"Canadian," Penelope breathed out. "Frank—*Pierre* is French Canadian."

"Ottawa to be specific, but close enough. His mother was Quebecois, hence the Frenchy first name. His Dad was...whatever the non-French version is. Hence Wilson."

"Where do you fall into this?"

He grinned, but his eyes remained deadly. She could also see how much he was straining to fight the pain from his leg and his wrist, which he cradled in his other arm. "Me? I'm American, born and raised."

"From Detroit, I presume?" Penelope offered.

His grin disappeared in a flash. "How the hell did you know that?"

Jane gasped beside her. "It was *you* he was sending money to?"

A wary expression came to his face as his eyes darted back and forth between the two of them. "He told me you didn't know nothin'."

"Assume we don't. Feel free to enlighten us," Pen said.

"Do you even have the silver button?" he asked with a scowl.

Penelope smiled. "Does it really matter now?"

"It matters," he muttered, seemingly to himself.

"Why?" Penelope asked in a sharp tone to reclaim his focus.

His eyes flashed to her in anger. When he didn't answer, she pointed the gun closer at him.

"You ain't got it in you."

"I do, but even if I didn't, I *do* have it in me to go upstairs and make a phone call to the police."

He grinned. "You think there's a phone in this house?"

"Fortunately I have a car I can drive to the nearest station."

He laughed. "You could barely drive the thing. Do you even know how to start it up?"

"I've seen it done. I think I can manage."

"Tell me more about Frank!" Jane said, brandishing the shovel. "How does he even know someone like you?"

"Your beloved husband ain't the saint you think he is. Where do you think all that money you have comes from?"

"He...sells Bibles," Jane said, but even Penelope could hear the uncertainty in her voice.

The man laughed, throwing his head back at the hilarity of it. "Yeah, I thought that one was a nice, ironic touch. I bet you ate it up, didn't you?"

This time Jane kicked him, but not in his injured leg. Still, it had the desired effect of ending the laughter and focusing his attention on them again, hissing in pain as he did.

"So where did the money come from?"

When he looked as though he was going to continue to be obstinate, Penelope decided to make it easy for him.

"We're going to turn you in to the police either way. There is no other way out for you. Besides, it's obvious that you enjoy causing his wife so much grief, why not deepen that cut?"

A slow smile spread his lips, making Pen realize she was right about him. The man was a monster and surely would have killed them eventually. She was glad she took a risk feigning that fall to get at the shovel.

"Diamonds, Lellouche Jewelers up in Toronto. Good old Pierre, or I guess it's Frank now? He was the one who masterminded the whole heist. And that certainly wasn't his first time—just his biggest score. That part was a bit of a surprise. For all his planning, we had no idea they had just got a shipment of diamonds in the day before. That's probably what made it all go to hell."

"My husband was a good and righteous man. He would never have been involved in something so...so..."

"Criminal?" The man cackled. "The Jesse James of Canada, you could call him." He suddenly scowled. "Except I was the only one who ever had the guts to pull the trigger. Yeah sure he had the smarts, could figure out a way into anything, but *I* was the only reason people buttoned up and paid out."

"What do you mean it all went to hell?" Penelope pressed, already having some idea.

"I mean, when we showed up, guns drawn, there were a few more people there than expected. I suppose that's why the lady behind the glass felt *plucky* enough to try and get mouthy and defiant. The stupid bit—"

"What did I say about watching your mouth in front of the lady?" Penelope said, giving him another kick, but only in the foot.

"The *polite old lady* took her time, so I shot her," he said with a sneer.

Both Penelope and Jane gasped in shock.

He seemed to enjoy that reaction so he continued. "And when the guy next to her tried to pull something, Frank, the bastard, tried to stop me from shooting him too. We fought and my gun went off. That scar on his face? Courtesy of yours truly," he said with a grin. "That pretty mug of his was no longer the same. Made him identifiable enough that he had to leave the country. Of course he got his, didn't he? I didn't even notice my button was missing until we went our separate ways."

"Why was Frank paying you?" Penelope asked.

"He had made good with his bit, investing it so's it grew

and all. I figured I might as well get a taste of it, seein' as how he wouldn't have had anything if it wasn't for me. At first, it was to protect that brother of his, the sorriest waste of space there ever was."

"Was?"

"Olivier, got himself snagged by the police. Some fight in a bar years ago, stupid kid. I thought they might like to know who it was they had in their possession, maybe extend his sentence. Of course, I could remain quiet for the right amount. Pierre was always too overprotective of the little jerk. Then again, those two didn't have much in the way of parenting so he practically raised Olivier himself. They wrote to each other almost every month while he was in the pen."

The boy from the picture in Frank's box. Now Penelope understood why part of the back of that photograph had been erased. Olivier was another French name, and his Canadian parents had probably spelled favorite as "favourite," on the back. The combination would have revealed his French-Canadian ancestry.

"Anyway, I made sure Pierre—sorry, Frank—knew that if he tried anything funny like killing me, a letter would be sent directly to the authorities about him. He never had it in him to be a killer anyway. He was fine ponying up the dough. At least until that useless brother of his got into another fight while serving his bit two-and-a-half years ago. Bumped off while serving time. Can you believe that?"

"Two-and-a-half years ago? But that's when..."

Penelope turned to Jane with a look of sympathy. She couldn't imagine what it must be like to learn your husband not only wasn't the man he said he was, but was something far worse.

He grinned Jane's way.

"I guess that's around the time you two started getting sweet on each other?" The man said with a grin. "For that, you have my eternal thanks. I thought all my blackmail material died along with that brother of his. I guess it was important to him that you didn't find out about his past."

"The money from the diamond heist wasn't enough for you?" Penelope asked.

He scowled at her. "I...made a few bad investments."

"Like that awful suit?"

She could tell he wanted to do a lot more than scowl at her now. After a momentary bit of enjoyment, she continued. "So, he sent you money every month, first because of his brother, then because of Jane?"

"You got it, lady. Except, after Olivier died, they realized who they'd had on their hands. That led to some renewed interest in the case. Frank was especially worried about being found out so he came out to Detroit to see me each month instead of using the wires. He knew the feds would be keeping an eye on those. Prohibition really ruined it for us legitimate crooks. Follow the money, or at least any record of it. That's how they caught those fellas down in St. Louis. Except this month he didn't show."

"How did you and Frank get involved with one another?"

"My mother was from Montreal. That's how I knew French." He glared at Penelope. "I spent some time up in Canada and happened to meet his brother after a bit of trouble with the local police. We shared a jail cell for a few days." He chuckled. "I knew he was useless even then, but that brother of his was someone who could be very useful. At first, Pierre wasn't interested in working with me. Bastard had the nerve to call *me* gaudy. Just because I happen to enjoy custom suits and nice things like that?"

"He probably knew it would get all of you into trouble. I'm guessing that's where the button comes in? Why would you wear a custom-made suit to a robbery? No wonder he didn't want to work with you."

"Well, we got the damn diamonds, didn't we? All thanks to me, by the way," he spat. "You think he woulda been able to retire if not for that job?"

"Perhaps you should have been as sensible with your money as he was," Penelope said, which only angered him even more.

"And you have no idea where Frank is now?" Jane asked, still sounding hopeful even after everything she'd learned.

"If I did, do you think I would have gone to the trouble of taking you two?" He grimaced as he looked down at his wrist and leg. "Look at me? I'm a mess! And my suit! That crazy broad put a hole in it!"

"Anything would be an improvement on that travesty," Pen said. "As for the rest, you well and truly deserved it."

"I shoulda killed you when I had the chance. I knew you two didn't know nothin'. All that wasted effort."

"Fortunately for you, we're happy to leave it to the authorities." Penelope turned to Jane. "I'm going to stay right here with the peacock, do you think you can find a phone somewhere nearby? In my purse is a card with the phone number for the 10A precinct. Ask for Detective Prescott and tell him who you are. He'll be happy to know you're alive."

Pen looked down at the man. "Where are we? The exact address."

"You think I'm gonna help you bring the police so they can—"

A nice kick, close enough to his bullet wound to have him screaming, and he gave up the address.

Jane gave him one last frown, then scurried up the stairs. Once she was gone, Penelope got settled back on the chair, with the gun still pointed at him.

"So Pierre is dead, huh?"

Penelope didn't bother answering him. He chuckled and shook his head, wincing in pain. He closed his eyes and seemed to settle back against the wall. "Well, it was good money while it lasted."

"Did he ever talk to you about Jane?" Penelope asked, hoping to gain some glimmer of positivity from all this. She had deliberately waited to ask when Jane was gone.

He squinted one eye open at her. "That topic of discussion was strictly off-limits. I tried asking about her once, seeing as he had a wedding ring and all. I thought he was gonna knock me to kingdom come."

So perhaps he really did want to protect Jane. Pen hoped she could at least take that much away from all of this, as broken-hearted as she must be.

"He traveled all the way to you just to give you the money?"

"Certainly didn't want me coming to New York. I appreciated that bit. I guess the Bible salesman thing was a cover story. How else could he explain making a living?"

Frank had a lot more to explain than that. In fact—

She stood up straighter as something occurred to her.

"You said he and his brother wrote to each other almost once a month?"

"Apparently. Back when I was first sniffing Pierre out for a little money. I knew I could find out where he was from Olivier. He had no idea what I was after, so he spilled. Told me he wrote to him in French since half the guards who liked to read the outgoing mail didn't know the language."

Penelope thought back to the box. There were no letters. If Frank loved his brother as much as this man claimed, certainly they would have been something he kept in the box. Maybe he didn't want Jane to know or ask about them back when he'd willingly shown her what was inside. She most definitely would have wondered about the French.

But where were they now?

Had the thief taken them? If so, why? What had they revealed?

More importantly, which of her suspects could read French?

"I tell you what though, if he ain't come back yet, he's for sure dead." The man grinned at her. "And whoever killed him, may just be comin' for you two dames just like I did. You think you can get lucky twice?"

"I think that's no longer your problem, mister."

CHAPTER NINETEEN

"Joseph Renwick Berry. Well-known thief and even more well-known for his...fashion," Detective Prescott announced.

"That's a very generous use of the term fashion," Penelope remarked. "Did you see his suit?"

She could tell by the look on the detective's face that he had no interest in discussing men's clothing styles. They were in the living room of the small house. It had been empty when he first broke in, thankfully. The resident was visiting family out of town this week.

Outside, the snowstorm had finally stopped, leaving a thick blanket of white that glowed in the light of the moon. Detective Prescott had, of course, called in the local authorities, but Penelope was glad he had still decided to come himself.

Even if the expression on his face did currently resemble her father's after the many times she had done something meddlesome as a child.

"Go ahead and scold me, you know you want to."

"I can't fault you for being taken against your will, Miss

Banks. Frankly, you handled it better than many policemen would."

"Why thank you, detective."

"But I trust you'll remove yourself from this case now? Allow the authorities to handle it?"

"Are they going to find out what happened to Frank Peterson? Or I suppose Pierre Wilson is his real name."

"He is still listed as a missing person."

"I'll take that as a no," she said, feeling indignant. "Even after all of this, and knowing that he was a wanted man, at least in Canada, they're still not giving it their full effort?"

"You explained it yourself. We've caught one of the men involved."

"You mean Jane and I have caught him."

He tilted his head and gave her a slightly exasperated look. "Only because you didn't heed my advice."

"You're welcome?"

He breathed out a soft laugh. "At any rate, if Frank is still alive, Mrs. Peterson will be happy to know that he has suddenly become a much higher priority."

"I suppose she'll want to change her name now." Penelope looked over toward the sofa where Jane was being seen by a doctor who had given her a light sedative. She'd been hysterical by the time she had managed to get in touch with Detective Prescott. Then the police had arrived and questioned her until she was a perfect mess. Penelope had finally had to step in and explain that Jane had known nothing about her husband, including his whereabouts, as proven by the fact that she had been hired to find him.

"Perhaps it will be some consolation that there was a ten thousand dollar reward involved. I suppose you could divide it."

She gave him a sardonic look. "It's hers. She's more than

earned it. I just worry about the publicity. She's already been through so much."

Detective Prescott's expression softened. "I'll do my best to avoid using her name, but this will be a big story. Not in small part because it involved a diamond theft that amounted to nearly five hundred thousand dollars."

Even divided three ways, it was no wonder Frank had been able to afford Winchester Court, on top of paying a little blackmail money. The amount didn't bode well for how hungry the press would be about this.

"I should go and talk to her."

"Of course," Detective Prescott said.

"Thank you for coming," she said with a smile. "I suppose I should find some way to show my appreciation?"

"It is my job, Miss Banks," he said, clearing his throat.

"Even after all we've been through together, it's still Miss Banks?"

He gave her a more daring look. "Until I have a reason not to use it."

Now it was her turn to clear her throat. Why? She wasn't sure. After all, she'd done so much flirting with him, it had all seemed like a game until now. He was just so handsome when he became forward this way.

"Well, I should...go see to Jane."

"Of course, Miss Banks." His mouth twitched ever so slightly and he rose.

She rose as well, casting one last subtle smile his way before going over to Jane.

"Is she able to talk?" she asked the doctor.

"She's fine. It's a mild sedative to calm her nerves, nothing too serious."

Penelope smiled and nodded, settling down on the couch next to her. The doctor gave them some privacy.

"How do you feel?"

"I'm not sure. I still can't believe it's true." She lowered her eyes and breathed out a soft laugh. "I suppose you think I'm silly and foolish, putting my faith in a man like Frank—Pierre. I believed all his lies. I have to question if he even loved me."

"Jane," Penelope said, taking hold of her hand and getting her attention. "That man went to an extraordinary effort to keep his past from tainting your marriage. In fact, he took an incredible risk to ask you to marry him in the first place, knowing what he'd have to go through to keep you happy. He could have continued living his life as a bachelor with his...yes, ill-gotten wealth, instead he chose *you*. Even Daisy commented on the fact that he never once looked her way. He only had eyes for you. And were you not happy?"

"Yes but..."

"But nothing. You can at least hold onto that much. There is also the reward money, which I think you've more than earned. Ten thousand dollars is nothing to dismiss."

"I can't reap the reward for what my husband did."

"*You* did nothing wrong. And *you* certainly deserve something to live on after all is said and done."

Penelope figured that Lellouche Jewelers and the authorities up in Canada would rightfully want whatever Frank, or Pierre had stolen, or the financial equivalent.

Jane's eyes went wide. "Will I have to claim it in person? I don't think I could do that, Miss Banks. What if there are reporters and—oh, my parents would find out! They warned me not to marry him. I knew I should have listened."

"Applesauce," Penelope scoffed. She'd always been a firm believer in defying one's elders when they spoke nonsense. In this case, perhaps Jane's parents had a point.

Still, her parents sounded positively atrocious. Besides, there was no denying she'd had a happy marriage while it lasted. "As for the money, I'll be the one to claim it, then give it to you in private. And if there are reporters, I'll handle them. Consider it all part of my services. It'll be a nice boon to my business. Finding a jewel thief? I'll be swarmed with cases."

She smiled encouragingly and Jane accommodated her with a small one of her own.

"You're too kind, Miss Banks. Do you think they'll leave me alone then? I can only imagine what Betty will have to say if she sees my name in the papers."

Penelope didn't have to imagine what her "friend" would have to say. "You just leave that to me. In the meantime, I'll have you put up at a hotel. How does The Plaza sound?"

"The Plaza?" Jane repeated, eyes wide. "Oh Miss Banks, I couldn't ask that of you."

"Applesauce. You've been through enough, I'm not about to throw you to the wolves as well. As I said, taking complete credit for all of this is my reward. I'll serve them up something quite delectable if only to give myself all the attention."

She thought of Lulu making up something for the press while still reaping the rewards. It was a fine idea as far as Pen was concerned.

Jane breathed out a small laugh. "You're too kind, Miss Banks."

"After everything that has happened, I at least deserve to be called Pen, or Penelope if that works for you. No need to be so formal."

Jane simply nodded.

"I'll ask Detective Prescott to take us back into town. I

trust him fully. But I'll need the key to your apartment so I can retrieve some of your personal items and a few changes of clothes."

"You think reporters are already there?" Jane asked, horrified.

Penelope thought they would soon be on their way *here* if they didn't leave soon, and it wouldn't take long for them to find out where Jane lived and wait for her there.

They'd just have to be disappointed.

"Don't you worry about that. You'll be comfortable at The Plaza, they know how to respect the privacy of their guests."

Jane nodded, flashing a brief, grateful smile. It quickly disappeared. "Do you think he was being honest? That he didn't kill Frank?"

Penelope twisted her lips in thought, then finally nodded. "He'd have been the sort of man to boast about it if he had."

"Which means he could still be alive?"

It almost broke Pen's heart to see the glimmer of hope in her eyes.

"Possibly? Either way, I plan on finding out." Despite what Detective Prescott might have to say about it.

"Really? Even after all of this?"

Penelope laughed lightly. "Oh Jane, this is hardly the first time my life has been in danger. Besides, I also promised Daisy I'd find her cat. I have a feeling it's connected."

"Lady is still missing? How terrible. But...you think it's connected?"

"Not directly, I don't think. But her cat did go missing around the same time as the burglaries started. She hasn't returned as she usually does, at least according to Daisy.

Who knows, maybe the thief *did* take her along with the valuables and the information that seemed to get Frank into trouble?"

The more Penelope thought about it, the more she was certain those letters from Frank's brother were in that box and had been stolen. Letters that could easily be used to blackmail him.

"Well, Lady certainly was a pretty thing," Jane said wistfully. "I can see why someone would want her. Even Mrs. Middleberry for all her complaints was always giving her little treats every time she purred past her door. I hope you do find her."

"The little minx had everyone around her finger—or rather paws, didn't she?" Penelope said with a laugh. "At any rate, the best place for me to keep looking is back at Winchester Court. I'll start first thing tomorrow."

Penelope would definitely get Leonard to drive her from now on. After today, she had to admit she was a bit shaken and it would be nice to have a man looking out for her. She doubted tomorrow's trip would be as enjoyable for him as going to the Silver Palace. No young ladies walking down *that* street would be bold enough to show their legs in this snowy weather.

Penelope sat up straighter and inhaled at a sudden thought.

"What is it?" Jane asked in alarm.

"I think I know what happened to Lady!"

CHAPTER TWENTY

"Does this mean you'll finally start taking advantage of my services? All it took was a little snow, huh?"

From the back seat, Penelope smiled at Leonard. "It was a bit more than that."

She hadn't told him or anyone else about yesterday's adventures with the diamond thief. Mostly, it was still to maintain Jane's privacy. Not being used to having a chauffeur after the past three years, when she'd had to rely on the subway or the bus, Penelope hadn't yet used Leonard's services enough to know if he was trustworthy.

"I hope I haven't taken you from anything else?"

He laughed. "Only another of Mrs. Davies's lunches with the ladies, as she calls it. I think she enjoys arriving in style."

Penelope smiled, remembering a time when her cousin thought cars were a sign of the end of civilization.

"I actually have you to thank for today's little investigation."

"Is that so?" he said with a grin. "Well, I'm happy to be of service. Care to tell me what it is I did?"

"I don't want to be insulting."

"Aw, now you really gotta tell me. I'm too curious. Don't worry about Leonard, miss, he's a tough old crow."

"You're only, what, thirty? Thirty-five?"

"Thirty-three, thank you very much. I feel like I've lived a long and interesting life. Miss Sterling wasn't a boring woman, God rest her soul."

"No, she certainly wasn't," Penelope said with a soft smile, taking a moment to look out the window at the snow. They were going through Central Park and it was still cold enough for the thick layer of white to cling to the ground and branches.

She took a breath, brightening back up, and turned to him with one eyebrow devilishly arched. "Did you have fun the other night after dropping Benny and me off at the Silver Palace?"

He turned to grin at her. "It was certainly better than yet another trip to a tea room."

Penelope laughed. "So you enjoyed the sights?"

He coughed. "Perhaps you could tell me what it is you're hinting at?"

"Tomcats. Not that you are one, per se. I'd hate to disparage your good name."

"Disparage away, just tell me how that helped you," he said with a laugh.

"It made me think about one cat in particular. She's very pretty and everyone adores her, particularly one very rascally cat."

"Okay..."

"I suspect she's...well to put it delicately, she now probably has a litter of kittens."

"Say what now?" He said, turning his head in alarm.

Penelope laughed and gave him a suspicious look. "Not to worry, I don't think any of them are yours."

"Well that's a relief," he said, exhaling a laugh and turning back around.

So, it seemed Leonard was *that* sort of man. Penelope wasn't one to judge, of course, she was a modern woman, after all.

"So we're going to pick up some kittens?"

"We're going to make sure they're okay."

They turned onto the street for Winchester Court and Penelope was dismayed to see that there were in fact reporters lingering outside. It proved she was right to book a room at The Plaza for Jane yesterday. She'd even used a different name for her to room under, just in case.

"I'm sure Mrs. Middleberry is positively loving this," she muttered.

"Let me escort you inside," Leonard offered, as he opened the door for her.

"Not necessary, I can handle myself with this bunch," Penelope said determinedly. She stepped out and lifted her chin. The sidewalks had already been shoveled so she quickly tried to make her way to the door. It was impossible. The reporters instantly crowded her.

"Are you a resident here? Do you know anything about your neighbor, Jane Peterson?"

"I have no idea who you are talking about. No one by that name lives here," she said, continuing on toward the door.

She realized her mistake was responding at all. The reporters were even more dogged in asking her questions now. "What about Frank Peterson? He's a resident here, her husband. How does it feel knowing you've lived next to a thief for almost two years?"

"The lady's answered your question, fella," Leonard said, forcing himself in between her and the reporters. He was a menacing enough presence to have them backing away.

Penelope was once again glad she'd thought to have him drive her. This was exactly the sort of nonsense he could be useful for. This, and avoiding getting kidnapped of course. She shuddered as she approached the door, thinking about what had happened yesterday.

"Are you alright, Miss Banks? Do you want me to come in with you?"

"I'll be fine once inside. Thank you, Leonard."

"Sure thing, Miss Banks," he said with a nod, then planted himself right by the door just in case.

Pen smiled as she used Jane's key to open the door and go inside. There was a separate key to get into her apartment. The foyer was empty and she headed directly for the door marked "Maintenance Only," pulling her hat off to get at one of her hairpins.

Before she could reach the door she heard the shrill voice of Mrs. Middleberry calling out.

Penelope sighed, then quickly made her way behind the staircase to hide. She noted that this was the perfect nook from which to look out and observe the entire foyer. Had this been where the thief hid and waited for people to leave the building?

"Miss Banks, are you down there? I just saw what happened outside." Mrs. Middleberry made it to the first floor, looking around in confusion.

"I could have sworn I saw her come in?" she muttered to herself. She headed to the front door to look out through the glass, and Penelope realized there would be no escape. With a sigh, she came from behind the stairwell.

"Mrs. Middleberry."

She spun around in surprise, hand to chest. She quickly overcame it in favor of indignation. "There you are. Isn't it an outrage? Reporters right out in front! As though this was some *criminal's* home!"

Penelope hoped by not responding, this undesirable conversation would quickly end. Unfortunately, Mrs. Middleberry was more than capable of filling the silence.

"I suppose you caught up with Jane?" She offered, peering hard at her. "They're saying that husband of hers was a jewel thief. The very idea! To think, I've been living across from them all this time. Who knows what could have happened, me here alone all day? He always looked like bad news, if you ask me. And a heretic too boot! I knew he was no Bible salesman. The police knocked on my door asking if I'd seen him recently. As if!"

"Hmm," Penelope hummed noncommittally.

"I suppose Jane is with him now?" she asked, scrutinizing Penelope. "The police are still up there searching the place. I suspect they're looking for the diamonds. I hope they find everything else that horrible man took from the rest of us. It was obviously him who stole my precious silver bowl!"

The police were still up there? That made escaping this insufferable woman slightly more difficult. It also meant she'd have to put off getting Jane's things.

Of course, it was no surprise. Frank had gotten away with a lot of diamonds.

"Mrs. Middleberry, does your husband know where you sneak off to every Tuesday and Thursday?"

"What?" That stunned her enough into silence.

"Your little secret?" Penelope offered. She was completely making it up as she went, but one thing she had learned was that no one liked others prying into their lives.

"I told you, I'm involved with the DAR."

"Really? So if I were to follow you, that's where you would be on those occasions?"

"How dare you insinuate something!"

"I just have my doubts is all. It must get awfully lonely being here by yourself all day. I wouldn't blame you if you sought out company every once in a while."

"*You* may be entangled with thieves and the harlots who marry them, but I am a God-fearing, honest woman, and I don't appreciate being accused of something I have no involvement with!"

Penelope simply stared, as though she still had her doubts. Blessedly, the outrage was too much for Mrs. Middleberry and she made her escape, but not before giving a few parting shots.

"I hope they arrest that Jezebel, wherever she is! She thinks she's too good to give nothing more than a hello? Serves her right."

Penelope reminded herself that Mrs. Middleberry was simply speaking out of anger, and people were prone to strike with an acid tongue under such circumstances. Still, she was glad to see the back of her as she stormed back up to her apartment.

Fortunately, the conversation hadn't drawn anyone else to the foyer. Pen plucked a pin from her bob and stalked right toward the door again.

This being her first attempt in the wild, so to speak, it took several minutes for her to work the lock. When it finally clicked open, she was stunned for a moment that it had actually worked.

Penelope quietly opened the door and snuck inside. The light was already on, which helped confirm her suspicions. The room was extraordinarily warm, being that this was where the boiler was. Still, it must be comfortable for the new mama and her kittens.

The sound of mewling filled the air and Penelope smiled, relieved that her hunch proved to be true.

"What are you doing here!"

She spun around to find Ana filling the doorway, not at all happy.

Penelope recovered from the small fright at being found out and narrowed her eyes. "Searching for stolen property. Which I suspect I've just found."

Ana's eyes went wide. "I have stolen nothing."

"Really?" Penelope said, tilting her head to listen better for the sound of kittens. "I think Daisy might think otherwise. Where is Lady?"

Ana's silence professed her guilt. She swallowed and hurried in, closing the door behind her.

"I did not steal cat!" she insisted, rushing past Penelope toward a far corner.

She followed Ana to see Lady, perfectly nestled in a large, flat basket stuffed with blankets. Beside it were two bowls, one filled with water, and the other had the remnants of some food. In the dim lighting, she counted five small heads in various mixtures of orange and white.

It seemed Pumpkin was officially a father. No wonder he was so excitable. By now he was probably already itching to start a new litter with another lady.

Men.

"I just keep her here until little ones grow is all," Ana explained, her accent becoming heavier now that she was excitable. "I see Lady walking down the hall and I knew something was wrong. I took her in, only to protect her while that one upstairs—" She waved a hand toward the ceiling and scowled. "—has her friends and her parties. When Lady finally has kittens, I bring her in here. Deyvid says we cannot take care of them all."

She bent down to stroke Lady and several of the kittens. She picked up one perfectly orange, furry kitten and smiled at Penelope as she cradled it.

"I had cat like this back home in Russia. Mila. That was before..." She took a moment to frown. "I had to leave her behind."

This at least explained why she was using the carpet sweeper so often. If she visited Lady several times a day, she probably carried cat hair everywhere she went. Anyone who saw the hairs would realize that Lady was somewhere in the building.

"All the more reason you should have at least told Daisy about Lady," Penelope said, not unkindly. "She's been worried sick."

"I know," Ana said with a sigh. "But, I fear she might take them back. That apartment is no place for new mother. There is party all night and they are always here. Daytime. Nighttime. Those people are always around. It never ends."

Penelope had to admit that the party she was at was no place for kittens who were only a few weeks old. She'd like to think that Daisy would have been responsible enough to put an end to them at least until the kittens were old enough. Ana obviously didn't have the same high opinion of her.

"All the same, we have to tell her now. Lady is hers and so are the kittens. I'm sure she'll let you keep one when it's old enough if you explain why you kept Lady here."

Ana seemed reluctant, but nodded and put the tiny kitten back. "Yes, you are right."

"I'll go with you, just to help her understand. Maybe help persuade her to give you another Mila."

Ana smiled fleetingly. "Yes."

Penelope followed her out, closing the door behind them. Then she led the way upstairs. Fortunately, Mrs. Middleberry was firmly ensconced behind her closed door, not daring to come back out again.

Pen knocked on Daisy's door and waited. When there was no answer, she tried again, louder this time, just in case she was deep in the sleep of too many White Ladies.

The door to Jane's apartment opened and a man emerged. He might as well have had "detective" printed on his forehead. Penelope was determined to ignore him. There was no reason to believe he'd know who she was based on sight alone. At least until Mrs. Middleberry's door also conveniently enough opened at the same time. She was more than willing to point the finger Penelope's way, literally.

"That woman over there, *she* knows the Petersons. She's close friends with them both. I wouldn't be surprised if she was in on the whole thing!"

Penelope sighed and attempted to focus her eyes on the door in front of her. At this point, she definitely didn't want Daisy to open it. No need to get her involved in this mess.

Her eyes landed on a dark red smudge near the doorknob.

"Is that...?"

"Miss?" The detective called out, walking over toward her.

Penelope was too focused on the smear which she was

now certain was blood. She straightened up and spun around to face him.

"Sir, I think this is blood on the door."

That of course got everyone's attention. Even Mrs. Middleberry exited her apartment and scurried over. The second detective left Jane's apartment and hurried to try and get ahead of her.

"I need all of you to stand back. Who lives here?"

"Daisy Fairchild," Mrs. Middleberry announced, then turned her nose up before adding. "She's a *dancer*."

The detective gave a few good knocks on the door and called out her name. "Miss Fairchild!"

When there was no answer, he tried the doorknob. It turned easily. Unlocked. That had the two detectives eyeing each other in a knowing way.

Penelope felt her stomach drop.

"I need you three to remain in the hall," he ordered before fully opening the door to enter. The other detective followed, both of them pulling out their guns.

That didn't stop the three women from craning their necks to see what lay beyond the open door. They all gasped in unison when they saw Daisy's legs as her body lay prone on the floor. The pool of blood confirmed something tragic had happened. The detectives rushed in, one kneeling beside her to check if she was still alive.

Although the two detectives spoke in hushed voices, the tone of it was apparent to everyone overhearing them.

Daisy Fairchild was dead.

CHAPTER TWENTY-ONE

Daisy had been stabbed to death.

Penelope was sitting in Jane's apartment with one of the detectives. They had originally wanted to take all three of them, Mrs. Klukovich, Mrs. Middleberry, and her down to the station. For once, Mrs. Middleberry's argumentative nature had worked in their favor. She had raised such a ruckus over the idea of being treated like a "common criminal" that they had compromised on interviewing the three of them here at the Winchester Court Apartments.

"So you were knocking on her door to tell her about a cat?" The detective confirmed, giving her a skeptical look.

"Her cat, Lady. It had gone missing and I was going to tell her it had been found."

"Down in the boiler room?"

"Yes." She hadn't told him the details about Ana essentially stealing the cat away while she nursed her kittens.

"How did you know the cat belonged to Miss Fairchild?"

"She mentioned it to me and I told her I would look for it. I'm a private investigator."

"Is that so?" She couldn't tell if his cynical expression was due to her professed occupation, being a female, or because she was "wasting" it chasing down a cat.

"It was part of a larger investigation into the string of burglaries that seem to have plagued the building. Are the police any closer to catching the culprit?" She asked, one eyebrow raised.

He gave her a slightly sour look, and she regretted being so impertinent. It wouldn't help end this interrogation any sooner.

"And you also know Miss Jane Peterson, the resident of this apartment."

"I do." There was no sense in lying.

"Were you also here today to visit her?"

"No, I was here about the cat." Perhaps a *little* lying was appropriate.

"Do you know where Mrs. Peterson is currently?" He gave her a hard, piercing look.

"I believe she's in a hotel somewhere. She's trying to avoid reporters. One wonders how they get their information so quickly." Not *necessarily* a lie. This time she felt no regret about her impertinence. It was obvious this detective was already suspicious of Penelope, being that she was entangled in so many different crimes.

The detective sighed. "Miss Banks, if you know anything about any of these crimes, it would be in your best interest to tell us. We're only trying to catch the perpetrators."

Penelope leaned forward. "So am I. Would you even be looking for Frank Peterson—or I suppose Pierre Wilson—if it wasn't for those diamonds? Frankly, if you'd done the work of finding him when his wife first came to you, who knows, maybe Daisy would still be alive."

"Do you think there's a connection?" he asked, even more suspicious now.

Penelope sighed and fell back. "I *do* know that there was a string of burglaries, after which Jane's husband went missing, along with Daisy's cat. My understanding is this thief obtained some information about who Frank really was and I assumed blackmailed him with the information. You should know he wasn't the only one being blackmailed. They also found out who Daisy's benefactor was, a Jameson; I suspect it's Jameson Dixon Martin. Perhaps you should be questioning him?"

She studied him to see if that elicited a reaction and was not disappointed. The detective's jaw twitched and he sat up straighter, giving her a wary look.

Now she was glad she hadn't brought up Detective Prescott's name as she had originally thought to do. The last thing she wanted was to get him into trouble.

"Excuse me for a moment," he said, rising up. She followed him with her eyes as he approached the other detective who had been interrogating a very concerned-looking Ana Klukovich. As an immigrant, especially one from Russia, she was probably far more worried about being mixed up in all of this.

The detectives were now probably debating how deeply to delve into Daisy's murder. At least without first discussing it with their superiors, who would no doubt run it up the chain of command to the Commissioner—and of course his good friend who went by the initials JD.

Pen feared Daisy's death might become a casualty of favoritism. That made her all the more determined to find out on her own who had killed her.

She frowned as she looked around Jane's living room which was a perfect mess thanks to their searching. Thank goodness she was safe in the hotel and didn't have to see the state of her apartment right now. Even the wedding photo had been knocked to the side.

Penelope stared at it, wondering if it was something Jane would want her to bring. She'd been so pleased with it the first time she'd shown Penelope, relating the story of how they'd met and then gone out together to look at the flowers.

She sat up straighter, her eyes focusing harder on the photo. A slow breath escaped her as something struck her.

"Daffodils."

Her eyes flicked to the detectives who were still huddled together in intense discussion. She flirted with the idea of telling them her suspicions but thought better of it. She'd had experience with incorrectly assuming a person's guilt before.

Frankly, she wasn't so sure that Jameson himself wasn't guilty of Daisy's murder. She had a feeling these two would be more than happy to pin the murder on anyone but him, even with what little evidence her brain was toying around with right now. No, it was best to be sure before she even mentioned a name.

"Detective, are we quite done?" she called out.

He turned to her with an irritated look, then walked back over. "At some point, I'll need to have a more formal interview with you back at our station. Until then, Miss Banks, I strongly caution you not to mention anything about this case—*any* of these cases—with anyone. Particularly reporters. Otherwise, I will have to arrest you for obstruction."

"I understand," she said in a perfectly accommodating tone, if only to help ease her escape. She cast a quick look toward Ana. "I assume you're done with all of us?"

"For now," he said, before turning to give Ana the same warning. She was even more appeasing in her assurances that she would keep quiet.

The two of them left Jane's apartment.

"Thank you, Miss Banks," Ana said with a note of relief in her voice.

"Of course," she replied with a smile. "I suppose you'll have to keep looking after Lady and her kittens for the time being."

"I will," Ana said happily.

They couldn't stay confined in the boiler room forever. At some point, the kittens would be weaned and anxious to roam. But Penelope couldn't concern herself with that now.

In the hallway, she could hear the outraged voice of Mrs. Middleberry through her door as she berated the detective brought in to interrogate her. With a small laugh, Penelope continued on and headed down the stairs to the first floor.

Outside, the reporters were more persistent than ever, having caught the scent of a new case, what with the influx of even more police. Pen just hoped they hadn't seen them remove Daisy's body.

Leonard was quick to come to her rescue yet again when the questions started up.

"Thank you," she said appreciatively as he guided her into the car.

"Where to now?"

"Just around the block if you will, then back onto this street again, and let me off at the cafe up ahead."

He turned to her with a befuddled look. "And here I thought driving you around was going to be as interesting as it was with Miss Sterling."

"You'll be happy to know this little ride may just help solve more than a few cases, including murder."

"Never a dull moment, Miss Banks, never a dull moment," he said with a small laugh before taking off.

CHAPTER TWENTY-TWO

Leonard let Penelope out at the corner of the street and she quickly slipped into the cafe. The same waitress who was there before saw her and her face lit up, no doubt remembering the nice tip she'd left last time.

"Hiya!" she greeted. "Another slice of apple pie? I can warm it up nice and hot for you."

"No, actually I was hoping to ask you about the last time I was here. You thought I was someone else?"

The waitress nodded. "Yes, from behind she looks just like you. Though I haven't seen her recently."

That must have been Daphne, no doubt ordering the usual recovery fare for a hangover after one of Daisy's all-night parties.

"You mentioned something about being surprised to see her here alone. Does she usually come with someone else?"

"A man," the woman said with a wry smile. "He usually comes in by himself though. Sits right at that table you were sitting at last time. I think he likes to watch people go by, he always stares out the window."

"Does he?"

"Mmm-hmm," she confirmed, nodding.

"Could you describe him?"

"Him? That one's a cake-eater, he is. He calls me Dandelion, even though my name's Susie. I guess 'cause of the blonde hair," she said with a sunny laugh as she plucked one of the curls of her permed bob.

Spanky. The man certainly seemed to love his flowers that started with the letter D.

"Thank you, Susie, you've been very helpful."

She pulled a five-dollar bill out of her purse and handed it over to an even more sunny Susie. It was money well spent.

Back outside, she quickly got back into the car before one of the reporters happened to look in her direction and see her.

"How would you feel about going back to the Silver Palace again?"

"I serve at the mercy of Miss Banks," Leonard said with a grin.

She sat back in her seat for the long car ride, thinking of the best way to approach this. She wasn't even sure if Spanky, or rather Spencer Ankara would be there, but it was the only place she could think of to find him.

It was a Tuesday, the same day of the week that Jane said Frank usually came home. Also a day of the week that there was no performance of the *Garden of Delights*. Which, meant no parties afterward at Daisy's place.

That was one of the things that sparked something in Penelope's mind. She found it hard to believe that Spanky had simply thought of calling Jane Daffodil out of the blue, which meant one of two things. One, he had been inside the

Petersons' apartment and seen either the wedding photo of her holding daffodils or had seen the silk flowers decorated around the room. Or two, he had overheard Frank calling Jane "jonquille," which meant he spoke French. Pen had heard him speak it at Daisy's party.

Which meant he could read every word of Frank's letters.

Combined with his habit of sitting at the cafe to watch Winchester Court—perhaps to see when certain people usually left for the day?—it made him the number one suspect as far as Penelope was concerned. Especially now that his star performer was leaving his "garden," and taking the police protection with her.

Or at least she would have if she were still alive.

Penelope sighed regrettably, realizing that Daisy would never make it to *Ziegfeld Follies*. There would be no more parties in her apartment. Lady would have to find a new home.

And all for what?

Did he kill her out of anger? Jealousy? Had she discovered he was the thief? Lulu had indicated that people only associated with the Silver Palace if they had no other option. Perhaps robbing the tenants of Winchester Court was Spanky's only option.

Either way, Penelope was determined to find out this afternoon.

The neighborhood surrounding the Silver Palace was far less impressive in the light of day. At night it had the atmosphere of a party, with strategically placed electric lighting that highlighted the best parts. In the sun, which seemed to glow even brighter against the glare of the snow, one could see everything for what it was. Even legitimate businesses like the shoe repair shop couldn't improve the setting.

"I'm thinking I should come in with you, Miss Banks."

"And I'm thinking you should stay with the car so it doesn't get stolen."

Leonard turned around. "You sure?"

"I'm sure. Worst case scenario no one answers and we'll be on our merry way. Best case, it's mostly dancers inside, hardly dangerous criminals."

"Save for one potential murderer?"

"You're certainly observant."

"Hard to miss the police presence back there at those apartments. I overheard enough from the reporters and coppers."

Penelope would have to use his services more often. He could be handy in the future.

"I'll be fine, Leonard."

Leonard let her out and she quickly went to the front doors of the theater. She knocked loudly, hoping someone was inside, perhaps even a maintenance person who she could bribe for Spanky's address.

It took several more knocks, and just when she was about to give up, someone opened the door.

"Whatdya want?" It was an older man with an expression that reflected his cranky disposition.

"I'm looking for Spanky. I have something important for him."

He eyed her up and down. "No more auditions, lady. Show's being canceled."

He almost closed the door in her face, but she stopped him. "It's not about that it's...a financial matter." Close enough to the truth.

Now he gave her a suspicious look, then cast another

more lingering look at her, no doubt noting how nice her coat was. "You got money?"

"I do if Spanky is in." Her frank tone seemed to speak his language.

"Ten dollars."

She laughed. "Five."

He grinned as though he had bested her and held his hand out.

"Only if he's in."

"He's in."

"How do I know?"

"You'll know for sure for five dollars."

"At least let me inside first."

He seemed to consider that, then shrugged and opened the door wider. Inside, with only the two of them as opposed to the crowd that was here last time, she felt the first prickles of danger.

"How about that five?"

She dug into her purse and pulled out a five-dollar bill and handed it to him.

He eyed the purse in a way she didn't like.

"You don't want to find out what else is in this purse," she said in as dangerous a tone as she could muster, despite her trepidation. "I also have my driver outside in case anything should happen to me."

He chuckled and shrugged, then shuffled along.

Penelope watched him go, breathing a bit easier.

"Well, are you comin' or not?"

She swallowed and followed him, keeping a firm distance between them. They went into the theater, which was completely lit up and looked perfectly revolting under the electric lights. Pen followed him up onto the stage and into the back. She gripped her purse, realizing this was completely stupid. Then, he reached a door and knocked twice.

"Someone here to see ya!" he shouted through the door.

Penelope heard grumbling on the other side and then the door swung open to reveal a less than debonaire-looking Spanky.

"Dammit, Carl—" He stopped when he saw Penelope. The transition was instant. A charming smile. A quick smoothing down of his shirt. Hair flicked out of his eyes.

"Our lovely Dahlia makes an appearance. To what do I owe the pleasure?"

"It's a financial thing," Carl said with a cackle as he shuffled off.

Spanky cast a suspicious look his way, then gave her an appraising look. "Financial?"

"I just said that to get inside."

He sagged, a look of irritation flickering across his face. "What is it then?"

"It's about Daisy." She paused, wondering how to broach this, and decided the unvarnished truth was the best route. If he'd killed her, he wouldn't be surprised. If he hadn't then...well, he would be. "She's been murdered. Someone stabbed her."

Penelope studied him closely to gauge his reaction. She needn't have been so perceptive, the surprise was obvious. Anguish immediately came to join it. Penelope felt the first seed of doubt in her mind but dismissed it. After all, he was in the theater so he knew how to put on a good performance.

"But...she was just here Sunday, doing her last performance," he said, staring off at nothing with a look of confused pain on his face.

"The police will be looking at you, being that you were a friend of hers."

"I was more than a friend, dammit," he snapped, running a hand through his hair. "Why would they think it was me?"

"Well, they know how often you were there at her apartment. Everyone knows she was your best performer and without her, the show might suffer, as you yourself said. There was also talk that perhaps the man who was paying for her apartment was keeping this show from being canceled?" she asked in a way that seemed to indicate she wasn't sure about it.

"The great and generous JD," he spat, a look of pure venom coming to his face.

"Did you know who he was?"

"I knew," he said, looking off to the side, suddenly numb. He blinked and snapped his eyes back to her. "How did you hear about her death?"

"I was there, visiting Jane when she was discovered," Pen lied.

"He didn't even know Daisy, not like I did," he said with a sorrowful expression.

"What made you think of daffodil for Jane?" Penelope decided to ask, being that she had just brought her up.

"What? I don't know," he said, giving her a distracted look. "Look, how do you know the police are looking at me for the crime?"

Penelope held back her impatience, putting on a facade of the concerned friend. "I heard them say your name," she lied.

"*My* name?"

"You were the producer of her show after all. You were always at one of her parties. Also, one of the residents has seen you at the cafe nearby, staring at the apartment during the day."

That seemed to startle him and Penelope felt some grim satisfaction.

"Listen...Mr. Ankara." She couldn't bring herself to call him something as ridiculous as "Spanky" under the circumstances. "I have money, it can buy a lot of influence. I would love to help you out if you truly are innocent. Perhaps if you could explain it to me? Your relationship with Daisy?"

His eyes narrowed with suspicion. "Why would you help me out? We barely know each other."

She realized that her facade was cracking. "Considering how important this JD might be, the police are going to want to close this case quickly and quietly and you make a perfect scapegoat. I'd rather they catch the *real* culprit. That goes for the burglaries too, which they certainly have enough evidence to pin on you as well. Better that than murder, no? Did you find out who was supporting Daisy when you robbed her? Did you try and blackmail him?"

"What? Why would I do that?"

"Because this show is closing down. You surely needed the money, no?"

"I loved her, dammit! I would never betray her like that...or *kill* her! *That's* why I sat inside that damn cafe with that irritating, meddling waitress, always popping up like a weed to bother me. Dandelion was the perfect name for that one. Despite myself, I couldn't stop watching for Daisy—during the day when I knew *he* wouldn't be there."

That explained a lot and created more doubt. Still, Penelope wanted to be sure.

"People often kill the ones they love, especially when the ones they love are with another man."

"You think that meant anything? She was just in it to

get to that damn Ziegfeld show and have a nice, swanky place to stay. We're all crooks, you silly dame. Grifters, con artists, lock pickers, even a pickpocket or two. Theater itself is the ultimate fraud." A sly look came to his face. "Something you might find you're a little closer to than you think, *Miss Banks*."

She frowned, not liking what he was insinuating. "The point remains, Daisy was leaving you, for something bigger and better."

"She was going to set me up with something once she was at the *Follies*."

"Is that what she promised you?" Penelope didn't bother to hide her skepticism.

He coughed out a hard laugh. "When I met her she was one of the best hustlers I'd seen. Pretty as...well, a daisy." He chuckled. "She'd cozy up to men, then cry foul, playin' like they'd done her wrong. For a few bucks, sometimes as much as a hundred, she'd shut up about it. Great acting that one. But not with me. We understood each other, *loved* each other."

Penelope thought back to meeting Daisy outside of her apartment. She seemed to indicate that Spanky was like Benny. Perhaps that was to cover for her real relationship with him.

"That's how I thought of this show," he continued. "All the better to lure them in. Married men don't want good girls, they want to be tempted by Eve herself. Jameson was almost too easy."

Penelope stood up straighter at his name.

He smirked. "Yeah, I've known who he was all along." His smirk disappeared and he slumped against the door frame. "I guess it doesn't matter now. Daisy's gone."

It was almost convincing, even with him admitting he

was essentially a con man. Still, she needed more, and in a way that wouldn't make him aware of what she was after.

"You might want to be less colorful when the police come calling, which they inevitably will."

A dry smile touched his lips but his voice was tinged with sadness when he replied. "I am, after all, a performer, Miss Banks."

She nodded. "Just one more thing, purely out of curiosity. Jane, how did you decide upon daffodil for her? Was it just because you seem to prefer flowers that start with a D?"

His brow wrinkled with consternation as though that hardly mattered.

"It was Daphne, I think. Yes, she was the first to mention it. *Jonquille*. Of course, she had to translate it for me. Grew up in Montreal, that one did. My French is quite limited. She seemed to find the woman amusing, perhaps because she was unlike the rest of us, plain and shy. Boring. Maybe it was the idea of someone like that being in our little production that sparked her amusement. She's like a cat that one, enjoys toying with timid mice."

Daphne.

Penelope had been so focused on Spanky, she had mentally pushed everyone else to the side. To be honest, Daphne almost blended in with the rest of the dancers who attended Daisy's parties, one with no special talent for dancing or singing.

Apparently, her talents lay elsewhere.

"Did anyone ever find Lady?" Spanky's voice drew her out of her thoughts. He still had no idea she suspected Daphne of killing Daisy. Penelope was surprised to see a tear come to his eye. She certainly hoped it wasn't part of a performance, but something told her it wasn't.

She smiled. "I did, she's safe."

He nodded, wiping the tear away with the back of his hand and standing up straighter with a deep breath. "Good. Daisy can at least rest easy knowing her cat is seen to."

That was something she would focus on later. Right now, she had to be sure Daphne was the real culprit.

And she knew exactly how to do it.

CHAPTER TWENTY-THREE

"Daphne Lavoie."

Penelope was with Jane in her hotel room that night. She was recovering from the news that Daisy had been killed. Although Jane hadn't been fond of her, she certainly hadn't wished death on the poor woman. The name of the potential perpetrator was enough to snatch her attention away from her momentary sorrow.

"Do you think she's the one who killed Daisy? Does she know where my husband is?"

Pen had remembered that Daphne's last name was French, but in the United States that hardly meant anything. She'd known Beaumonts, Chevrolets, Tremblays, and more who couldn't speak a lick of French.

"I think she knows something. Did you ever have any interactions with her, anything that comes to mind that might make you suspicious in retrospect?"

Jane seemed to think about it. "I mostly avoided Daisy's friends. Though—" She sat up straighter.

"What is it?" Penelope asked.

"She did remark one day on my husband's scar. She

mentioned how scars always made men seem dangerously attractive and asked if that's what drew me to him. She seemed to be suggesting something about him, so I didn't respond. I could hear her laughing about it as I quickly left. Now, I wonder if she knew."

"When was this?"

"It was months before the burglaries, which is why I didn't think it was related. It wasn't as though my husband's scar was a secret. It's apparent to anyone who sees him."

"Maybe she did a little investigating of her own and knew exactly what to look for among your husband's things. If she's from Montreal, she knew what he was saying when he called you jonquille. Maybe his accent gave away that he was from Canada? Then when she finally had reason to break in she must have found some proof of something—like a silver button. Or the letters written in French?"

"And you think she blackmailed him?"

"That's the obvious conclusion."

"So what happened? He was already being blackmailed by that other horrible man, why would this be different?"

"Something obviously went wrong. Maybe that explains why Daisy suddenly lost favor with Jameson. Maybe Frank was no longer a viable option so—" She quickly flashed an apologetic look Jane's way.

"It's fine, Miss Banks. At this point, I've come to accept that he's dead. I just want to know what happened. Then, maybe I can move on."

"I think that's a healthy way of looking at it."

"So, Daphne could no longer use Frank as a source for blackmail and she switched to this Jameson? But why kill Daisy?"

"That's what I have to find out. It may also explain why

Frank is missing." She thought about what Spanky had said. "I don't think Daphne likes to play nicely."

"Perhaps the police should handle this. If she's that dangerous, I'd feel terribly guilty if something happened to you just because you were still looking into what happened to Frank."

Penelope smiled. "Don't worry, I'll go to Detective Prescott first. I trust him."

"He's a very nice man. He was so calm and patient with me on the phone."

"Detective Prescott? He's hardly ever that way with me," Penelope said with a frown. Then again, she didn't have Jane's temperament.

Jane gave her a knowing smile. "He's handsome too. But then I suppose I have a slight bias for men with scars." That seemed to cause a sudden bout of sorrow in her and her face fell. "I suppose I'll have to go to the police again at some point, before they find me. I'm sure they suspect me of something."

"Not before I find out what happened to your husband. You at least deserve that bit of reassurance before you go put yourself through that misery."

Jane nodded.

With that settled, Penelope stood up. "In the meantime, I'm going to talk to Detective Prescott. With everything I've learned from Spanky and what you've told me, that should be enough to at least have Daphne brought in for questioning."

"Do you think she'll reveal what happened to Frank?"

"Let's hope so," Penelope said optimistically. Inside, she was far more pessimistic. If Daphne was as unsavory a character as Spanky implied, this was going to be a difficult case to solve.

"They *what?*"

Penelope was with Detective Prescott later the next day inquiring about what had happened with Daphne. She had been thoroughly outraged to learn that the police had let her go after questioning.

"There simply wasn't enough to hold her on."

"Even after everything I told you?"

"All circumstantial evidence, if that. She's been to Daisy Fairchild's apartment multiple times, so fingerprints are useless. Even the ice pick used to murder her, she claims several witnesses can attest to the fact that she used it at her last party to make drinks."

Penelope exhaled with frustration, realizing even she could be a witness to that fact, having been to said party.

"She even allowed the police to search her apartment. There was no sign of any of the stolen goods."

"Well of course she wouldn't keep them there, she probably has them hidden away somewhere, if she hasn't already sold them for money. Is this because of Jameson Dix—"

"Miss Banks." Detective Prescott gave her a hard look.

"You might as well take me back into the interrogation room again, because I fully plan on speaking my mind, completely uncensored."

His nostrils flared with anger, but he rose. This time he didn't bother taking her hand—a disappointment to be sure—as he stormed toward the same room. Penelope trailed him at a stubborn distance, filled with her own bit of righteous anger.

Once the door was closed, they both spoke, or rather shouted, at the same time.

"Just because some big, important man has the entire police force in some kind of chokehold—"

"The police can't simply arrest someone based on your hunches and assumptions—"

"You're willing to let justice be denied—"

"This isn't some fascist regime where we can hold people without any proof—"

"Never mind that there is still a missing husband, no doubt dead—or does that not matter anymore?"

He was the first to stop talking, exhaling with impatience as he ran one hand across his dark hair.

"This isn't helping."

"I agree, Detective Prescott. You've made some very salient points. I should take my leave."

He studied her with unveiled suspicion.

"Absolutely not."

Penelope's brow rose. "I have no idea what you're talking about."

"Yes, you do, and no, I'm not allowing you to talk to Jameson, Miss Banks. You're already in enough trouble as it is."

"Am I?" she asked innocently.

"Yes, and therefore, so am I. I have at least two other departments—hell, another country!—calling my commanding officer, wondering why it is I'm involved in something that is well outside the jurisdiction of this department."

"I would think they'd be serving you a medal! You helped apprehend a wanted jewel thief and closed one missing person case. You also heroically came to the rescue of two damsels in distress." The detective couldn't help a slight twitch of the lips at that one, especially with the overly fawning intonation she added. "You're nearly on the verge of catching a burglar and possible killer, while at the same time closing another missing person case. Oh, and we found Lady, Daisy's cat."

"Well, bully for you, Miss Banks. I'm sure the entire police force of Manhattan will sleep better knowing that the cat was found."

"As they should! It's all quite adorable as it turns out. She had kittens, five total and they're all a mixture of white and—"

"Miss Banks," he interrupted in a terse voice, sounding perfectly exasperated.

Penelope pursed her lips and went silent, patiently waiting for him to rant once again.

Instead, he studied her with a vexed expression. "There is nothing I can say to stop you, is there?"

"You know it's the only way to get a definite answer. Jameson could be the one link revealing Daphne as the blackmailer, and thus the culprit in all of this. If she's already contacted him—"

"*If.*"

"Then he can admit it and then you have your guilty party. She's desperate, detective. Frank is most likely dead. Jameson is her last chance. If we can get him to reach out to her, pretend to offer her money to keep her quiet, it may just work."

"What makes you think he'll play along?"

Penelope twisted her lips and averted her gaze.

"*You're* going to blackmail him? I should have you arrested right now."

"Not blackmail, just...extreme persuasion."

"That sounds an awful lot like blackmail."

"Only because you're an honest officer of the law," she said prettily.

"When have your attempts at flattery ever worked?"

She gave him a coy look. "I'd like to think they've worked at least a little bit in the past."

Much to her pleasure, he colored ever so slightly. But there would be time for flirting when this was all over. Hopefully, by then he'd be at least thanking her. For now, she needed to plead her case.

"Detective, a woman is dead, and quite possibly a man," she said in a somber tone. "For all we know Jameson himself killed her."

"Is that what you believe?"

"Not really, I think Daphne is responsible for it all. Which is why I feel so strongly about this. People's lives have been ruined. People's lives have been *taken*. You know the department isn't being as thorough as they should be in handling this. To them, Daisy was nothing more than a dancer in some seedy show. Easily brushed away. They're far more worried about offending the wrong person than arresting the right person. I don't have those same constraints holding me back."

"That's what concerns me."

She gave him a dry smile. "I don't plan on charging in like a reckless bull. I've learned my lesson about that. I am capable of a delicate touch."

She noted his eyes blink twice in rapid succession before he cleared his throat.

"Besides, I have something the average policeman doesn't to lure him in," she said primly.

Detective Prescott's eyes widened in shock.

Penelope exhaled with amused indignation. "*Money*, Detective Prescott," she said smartly. "And plenty of it."

He visibly relaxed, then gave her a stern look. "I can't condone this."

"Naturally."

"Nor can I prevent you."

"Also true."

He sighed. "Will you at least promise not to put yourself in danger?"

She pretended to think about it for a moment. "I'll try."

Detective Prescott didn't look at all amused.

"Don't worry, detective, I still have your number if I need help," she said with a smile as she walked out.

CHAPTER TWENTY-FOUR

The thing about men like Jameson Martin was that they were far more inclined to use weapons that killed you socially, politically, and financially rather than physically.

Fortunately, that was a world Penelope had grown up in, and thus, she had better ammunition. New Money was certainly a force to be reckoned with. It was often far more robust than old money, which tended to wane once the third or fourth overly-entitled generation got its greedy hands on it. It was also full of vim and vigor and, more importantly, an unhealthy amount of pride, often to its detriment.

Jameson had greased all the right wheels to not only make a name for himself, but also swaddle his interests with a good degree of protection. But he was still a prideful man. He'd probably been an easy mark for Daisy, who no doubt fluffed his feathers in just the right way.

Penelope had called to make an appointment regarding an ambiguous "Banks family business interest." The Banks family name held some sway. Never mind that, according to the feelings of her father, Penelope had only brought shame to that name. Still, it was enough to grant her a meeting.

The look he met her with was curious but guarded.

Pen wouldn't have been surprised if her name had been forwarded to him as part of this investigation. Being that she had her own money, he would know she wouldn't be here to blackmail him. But it would have been stupid of him to not at least find out what she wanted.

"Miss Banks, have a seat."

She took a seat and considered him with a frank look.

"I won't waste your time with too many pleasantries Mr. Martin. I've come to ask a favor of you, a somewhat delicate one, admittedly, but highly important all the same."

"Ah," he said, relaxing with a knowing smile. "You've come to beg money for some charitable cause or another. My wife is positively draining me right now, helping orphans or widowed mothers or some other such nonsense, but I suppose I can open the coffers a bit more for yet another cause."

"Not to worry, Mr. Martin, I haven't come to ask money from you, at least not directly. I was hoping instead you could get in touch with someone."

His brow wrinkled in confusion. "Some sort of letter of introduction? From me?" His chest puffed out and an absurdly pleased smile came to his face. "Miss Banks, I believe we know all the same people, and surely your father—"

"With the person who's been trying to blackmail you."

His face went ashen and his chest seemed to contract as he fell back into his seat.

"I'm not asking you to pay them off, just organize a meeting. We simply need to confirm the blackmailer's identity."

"We?" he asked in alarm.

Penelope chose her words cautiously, realizing that he was about to flee like a panicked deer. Or rather, ask her to leave before she got what she wanted.

"Right now only I and a few others know about this. I'm fine keeping it that way. At the very least, think of Daisy."

"Daisy knew to keep her mouth shut. That was my only requirement. I got her letter trying to make it up to me, but...I suppose that no longer matters. Her troubles are no longer my concern."

"Troubles?" Penelope repeated incredulously. "She's *dead*, Mr. Martin, not...suffering gambling debts."

"And I'm very sorry about that, but it's all the more reason I can't get involved. There's nothing to be done for her now. I, on the other hand, have a wife and children to think about."

"You didn't seem too concerned about them when you put her in that apartment."

His gaze narrowed. "I think it's time for you to leave, Miss Banks."

He rose, encouraging her to do the same.

Penelope remained seated.

"As I said, Mr. Martin, right now only I and a few others know about this," she hinted.

"How would your father feel knowing what you've gotten yourself mixed up in?" He said in a threatening voice.

Penelope laughed airily. "Oh, I don't think he'd be surprised at all. By all means, give him my regards if you do decide to tell him."

Not for the first time, Penelope relished how enjoyable it was to be unbridled by "decent" society. It left one with so few scruples that interfered with a peaceful existence—or a murder investigation.

Jameson exhaled and sneered. "Ah, yes, that's right. I'd heard there was some trouble with you. Something about a man. I see now that the rumors are true. You're just like your mother aren't you?"

Penelope sucked in a breath and glared at him.

He smiled, realizing he'd finally managed to create a small crack in her confidence. "Though at least she had the sense to use her wanton tendencies to create interest and popularity, even if it was of a prurient nature. Not that I was ever invited to one of her sordid dinners."

"She *was* rather particular."

He took that as the insult it was intended to be.

"You've just made yourself a dangerous enemy, young lady."

Penelope simply smiled. "Mr. Martin, that threat doesn't scare me. It didn't when I was poor and it certainly doesn't now. In fact, anytime I hear a man threaten me with one thing or another, I know I must be doing something right."

"We'll see how you feel once I'm done with you. If you breathe one word about this to the press or anyone else, I will make it my mission to destroy you."

Penelope tilted her head. "The way you did Daisy? Was it you who killed her?"

He blustered for a bit, practically seething. "How dare you! That is a vicious lie and one I will not tolerate!"

Funny, he hadn't claimed anything else she'd mentioned was a lie, which made her think this was true. Still, it could be good leverage.

She stood up. "A shame then, since it's far more likely that this blackmailer of yours committed the act. If only the police could place Daisy's murder on the shoulders of the young woman who is blackmailing you."

"That's assuming they even know this young woman exists," he said in a sly tone, then smiled darkly. "I doubt she'd go to the police herself and confess."

Penelope studied him. He hadn't so much as blinked at the idea that his blackmailer was a young woman, which confirmed that it was. Men like him usually balked at the suggestion that a woman, especially a young one, could do anything more than have babies or sew needlepoint.

A smile cocked on one side of her mouth. "If you think I'm a problem for you, Mr. Martin, I'd caution you to be far more concerned about this woman. She's killed at least one person, perhaps two. She has nothing left to lose, which makes her quite desperate and, worse for you, quite dangerous. If I were you, I'd prefer her in prison, especially if you, as you so endearingly put it, want to protect your wife and children."

Something ghosted across his face. Fear?

Penelope waited, if only to see if it would persuade him to do the right thing. However, it disappeared, replaced by resentment and anger once again.

"It's time for you to take your leave, Miss Banks."

"Fine then, Mr. Martin. Good luck."

She kept her head held high as she left, but couldn't maintain it by the time she exited the building where his offices were located. Back on the street, the snow around her still clinging to life, though by now covered in dirt and muck, she felt her frustration kick in.

"Pineapples," she spat. A man passing by gave her a strange look, which she ignored.

Jameson had at least confirmed that his blackmailer was

a young woman. He'd all but pointed the finger at Daphne. Penelope just had to find a way to find evidence against her.

As it was, she would no doubt be receiving a harshly worded phone call from her father, berating her for being the wild child that she was, once again wreaking havoc. That thought at least put a smile on her face. It was enough to spur her on.

Something would come to her. It always did.

CHAPTER TWENTY-FIVE

PENELOPE HAD LEONARD DRIVE HER BACK TO THE Winchester Court Apartments later on that day. This time, she did intend to pick up a change of clothes for Jane and retrieve some other items. She was surprised to see one reporter still standing outside. He was young, thus probably eager for his shot at something big.

"You are persistent, aren't you?"

He grinned. "You have something to offer about the diamond heist?"

"I most certainly do not," she scoffed and was about to continue on her way, then stopped and turned back to him with a considering look. "But I may have something just as tasty in a while. An exclusive. A reward for your doggedness."

"Really?" He brightened up.

"What's your name? What paper are you with?"

"James—Jimmy McDuff," he told her, giving her a card. "Anything you got, I'm willing to take, miss."

Penelope looked at the card with his information, including the name of the paper he was with. She figured it would be a good idea to get business cards of her own. Yet another thing to add to her list of occupational necessities.

"I have to warn you, your superiors may not like the story. It involves a *very* important and well-connected man." She waited to gauge his reaction. The fire that lit up in his eyes was all the confirmation she needed that perhaps there were still honest papers out there. Or at least those that saw the value of profit over favoritism.

Pen smiled and continued to the door. She unlocked it with Jane's key which she had held onto. She came to a stop when she stepped foot in the foyer, the door closing behind her. Her gaze dropped to the keys in her hand.

"How did she get in and out of the building?"

During Daisy's parties, it would have been easy enough for Daphne to be let in. Frankly, anyone walking in off the street would have been happily and quite tipsily allowed ingress. But what about during the daytime, long after most of the partygoers had gone home? Also, the parties were only ever held after performances at the Silver Palace, which ran Thursday through Sunday.

The observant eyes of Mrs. Middleberry and Adam Pulley would have prevented Daphne from lingering near the front door long enough to wait for someone to open it. Using her raised voice to call Daisy to let her in through the tube system would have alerted them as to her presence. As for picking the front door lock, even an expert would be dumb to try that in broad daylight.

It was yet another mystery to solve.

"One thing at a time," Penelope said to herself.

She continued up the steps. On the second floor, she could hear the muffled sound of Ana's carpet sweeper above on another floor. Pen continued toward Jane's apartment.

Pen quietly turned the key in the lock, not wanting to

alert Mrs. Middleberry to her presence. Blessedly, she made it inside without the door to 2A opening. Perhaps Pen had forever ruined any goodwill with the woman after their last encounter. Thank goodness for that.

Once inside the apartment, her eyes fell to the windows that, in this unit, faced the back. Penelope rushed over and looked out. It was the perfect exit. Penelope remembered looking out during Daisy's party which also faced the back. With no lighting, it was pitch black, great cover for an escape—especially in a panic after committing murder.

But the second floor was too high to jump from without risking an incapacitating injury, especially in the dark.

Looking out at the yard right now, it was obvious someone had been back there. Penelope noticed the footprints in the snow that led directly to the back gate. However, even from this distance, she could see that they were too big to be Daphne's. Otherwise, it was mostly animal prints, probably a squirrel or stray cat—

Penelope stood up straighter.

"That's it!"

She ran from Jane's apartment and down the hallway to the window that led out to the fire escape. Pen tugged on it, and sure enough, it was unlocked. It hadn't even made a sound. Mr. Kluckovich kept it running quite smoothly.

Daphne could have easily unlocked it during one of Daisy's parties. That would make it easier for her to sneak back into the building from the back without having a key. Based on what Spanky had said, she was probably an expert lock-pick or pickpocket, which would have helped her either pick her way into an apartment or temporarily steal a set of keys.

After finishing her robberies, all she'd have to do was walk out the front door. Working in the theater, she was a master of disguise. Even Penelope hadn't recognized her on stage with all that makeup and a wig. Most of the things that were stolen were small enough to fit into a woman's bag, or simply put on, like Daisy's fur coat.

Penelope still had on her coat so she pulled the window up and climbed out onto the fire escape. She could see that the ladder was lowered enough for someone to easily reach it from the ground if they were trying to get back in. She looked out into the small yard from her vantage point. She could see that some of the prints she thought were animal prints were actually the heeled portion of a shoe. It followed a more circumspect path along the border of the yard, which was why she hadn't had a clearer picture of them before.

This meant Daphne had been here sometime after it had started snowing. Daisy had still been alive to perform Sunday night according to Spanky, and Monday the snow had started. It had stopped that evening. On Tuesday, Daisy's body had been found. That meant these prints had been left within the window of Daisy's death. Perhaps that night under the cover of darkness?

The yard was shielded from the sun by the buildings surrounding it. That plus the continuously frigid temperatures had maintained the snow and kept it from melting even a little.

And it had preserved the footprints.

Penelope felt her heart quicken as she followed the footsteps with her eyes. As much as she wanted to go down and get a closer look, she knew that it would compromise the scene.

At some point, Daphne's prints changed, as though she had slipped and maybe hurt herself. The snow was disturbed in that area, confirming that idea. The remaining prints seemed to favor one leg since there was only a single heel imprint from that point on.

Penelope eyed the disturbed area, her attention caught by something red. She made her way down the ladder to the bottom rung to get a better look without actually stepping onto the snow.

That's when she saw it. A red heel with black sequins. It was hidden underneath a small, dead garden shrub.

She gasped at the sight of it. That's why Daphne's footprint had changed. Her heel had broken, perhaps when she slipped on an icy patch. She had probably worn the red shoes that night when coming to visit Daisy for whatever reason. By then, all the sidewalks in front had been shoveled and salted. If the murder hadn't been premeditated she wouldn't have thought to wear something that would make it easier for her to escape through the back covered in snow and ice.

Penelope grinned and quickly scaled the ladder again to go inside. That's when her eye absently landed on the gate secured with a padlock.

"Pineapples," she said with a frown, coming to a stop.

The lock posed a definite problem with her theory as to how Daphne had both entered and escaped the yard. She looked at the wooden fence surrounding the yard. It was too tall to climb over. That worked in keeping thieves out, but it also created the problem of keeping thieves—and murderers—stuck inside. Besides, how would she have relocked it once she was on the other side of the gate?

Pen glared at the lock, as though she could wish it away. She tilted her head to consider it. It hadn't been there when she'd first come to Jane's apartment last week. It looked new. Perhaps it was? As in, put in *after* the murder of Daisy Fairchild?

Penelope perked up, wanting to hurry back inside to confirm. She followed the sound of Ana's carpet sweeper to the third floor.

"Ana!" she called out. It took several tries before she got the woman's attention over the noise.

"Miss Banks," she greeted with a smile, turning the machine off to greet her. "The kittens are doing fine."

"Wonderful," Penelope breathed out. "I actually have a few questions, though perhaps your husband might be better able to answer them."

At the panicked look on her face, Penelope hurried to reassure her. "It's nothing bad. I just wondered about the lock on the gate in the back. When did it get put on?"

"It was the evening after..." her eyes lowered. "After Miss Fairchild was found."

Penelope kept herself from grinning at the confirmation that her hunch was still correct. "Why was it put on then and not before?"

"Well, after the murder, everyone is so scared and worried. Also, Miss Seymour in 3C claims she heard stray animal in yard that night. She worry about her cat—rabies. So, Deyvid, he put lock on to reassure everyone."

"Of course," she said with understanding. "Thank you, Ana."

Ana smiled and continued sweeping the floor as Penelope hurried back to Jane's apartment.

It all made sense now. Daphne had tried escaping through the back under the cover of darkness the night she killed Daisy. She had slipped on the ice and broken a heel. In the pitch-black darkness, she had probably made noise looking for it. Mrs. Seymour had no doubt opened her curtains to investigate, scaring her off before she could find it. She had probably meant to come back to search for it the next day, but by then the lock had been put on keeping her from getting in.

In Jane's apartment, Penelope used her phone to call her favorite detective. When she was finally put through to him, she couldn't keep the grin from her face.

"I have proof Daphne killed Daisy."

CHAPTER TWENTY-SIX

"It is very convincing, I have to admit," Detective Prescott said as he stood on the fire escape with Penelope, looking at the prints and, more importantly, the heel in the snow. He had brought the police photographer who was now taking pictures of everything.

"Obviously not enough for the original detectives. They certainly didn't bother being very *thorough* in their investigations, did they?"

Detective Prescott tactfully refrained from responding, but Penelope could see the flash of anger in his eyes.

"Well, they'll have no choice but to start looking into this now, won't they? Even JD won't be able to put the kibosh on this one! Thank goodness Daisy has someone looking out for her."

"Very good, detective." Detective Prescott looked at her with a degree of admiration. He rubbed his chin. "The thing is, this heel, unless the shoes were custom made, we can't claim it's hers."

"They're obviously her favorite, she wore them all the time. Several people can attest to that. You have no idea how much a woman will value her favorite shoes, detective, especially one who doesn't have much money."

"And that will certainly help build a case against her, but without more, it's still weak."

Penelope thought it was slightly more robust than that, but she could see how a case like this would need to be airtight, especially if they were to get around the protections of one Jameson Dixon Martin.

If she could prove definitively that these were Daphne's shoes then they'd have to at least arrest her. It planted her right here around the time Daisy was killed. Pen thought back to when she had first seen Daphne in the shoes, the strap caught between her teeth as she buckled the other one onto her foot.

"The buckle!"

"What is it?" Detective Prescott said, noting her excited expression.

"I think I know how to prove the shoes were hers. Let's go."

She practically dragged him back to the front of the building. Outside the young reporter, Jimmy brightened up at their reappearance.

"You're a detective right?" Jimmy said, using his keen reporter's sense to state the obvious. "Any new developments?"

"No comment," Detective Prescott said in a terse voice.

Penelope was far less inhibited. "You stay right there and if my hunch is correct, I will give you the story of the year."

The smile on his face grew.

Now, it was Detective Prescott's turn to drag her away.

"Are you trying to get yourself into even more trouble?"

"Trouble might as well be my name," she happily said as

they approached the car where Leonard immediately jumped to open the door for them.

"The Silver Palace," Penelope instructed, causing her chauffeur to grin.

Detective Prescott gave her an uncertain look but didn't argue. When they finally arrived, Penelope was so eager, she didn't wait for Leonard to open the door for her.

"If you're going in there, I'm going in first," Detective Prescott said, hurrying after her.

"Not the theater," she said with a grin as she looked both ways before crossing the street. "The shoe repair shop."

"Huh," Detective Prescott said, staring at the shop with understanding as he followed her.

Penelope opened the door to the shop, the legitimate one that was currently open for legitimate business. One of the men behind the counter was the same one who had escorted Benny and her to the nondescript door to his right, behind which was a speakeasy establishment.

If he recognized her, he was wise enough not to make note of it. Though she suspected after today, having brought in the police and all, even Benny's password wouldn't gain them entry in the future. If it helped find Daisy's killer, and possibly Frank's, she didn't care. There was a speakeasy hidden away on every street in the city.

Pen's eyes scanned the walls looking for one pair of shoes in particular.

"There," she announced, pointing at a red pair that sat on a shelf behind the counter. One had a missing heel. "Never underestimate the way a woman feels about her favorite pair of shoes, detective."

Detective Prescott took charge from there, pulling out

his badge to show the two men. They eyed each other warily, visibly tensing.

"I need to know who those red shoes belong to, a name and address."

The two of them relaxed only slightly, no doubt wondering if this was some ploy to uncover their illegitimate side business.

"Or, I could come back with a warrant and perform a more *thorough* search of the premises?" Detective Prescott said in a knowing tone.

Even Penelope gave him a look of surprise. How did he know?

Still, she knew from past experience that he had no interest in arresting people for illegal alcohol, perfectly willing to leave that business to the feds.

"I, uh, have the slip right here," one of the men said, quickly opening his book to pull it out. "Daphne Lavoie. She's one of the performers from across the street. They come here a lot to get their shoes fixed."

"When did she bring this pair in?" Detective Prescott asked.

"It's right here on the slip, Tuesday."

Penelope gave Detective Prescott a satisfied smile. "Good enough for you?"

"Certainly good enough for another round of interrogation, much more thorough this time."

"I have a better idea," Penelope said with a grin.

CHAPTER TWENTY-SEVEN

"Hello again, JD!" Penelope sang out, after flying past the secretary and through to Jameson's office.

"I'm so sorry, Mr. Martin," his visibly flustered secretary said, running after her. "Shall I call security?"

"Oh, by all means do, I think they should hear this," Penelope said with a smile, giving him a questioning look.

His red face struggled with the conflict he felt before he waved his secretary away, "It's fine, Bertha. Close the door will you?"

Bertha gave Penelope a withering look before following his orders.

"I already told you, Miss Banks, I'll have nothing to do with this."

"But you haven't even heard my offer," Penelope said with mocking disappointment in her voice as she casually took a seat across from him.

"I don't care to know what your offer is. Now please leave."

"Really?" she pressed, squinting one eye at him.

"Because we have a *very* strong case for murder against your blackmailer."

"Well, then, I suppose you don't need me," he said with cautious satisfaction.

"The thing is, it's still not *quite* good enough. I happen to know the woman and she'll be very likely to take her chances with a trial. A very *public* trial. What with the involvement of a diamond thief, the burglaries, the two murders, and the, um, *Garden of Delight* at the Silver Palace, well, you know how much the press loves those kinds of sordid details."

His jaw tightened in anger.

"I, for one, plan on offering myself up as a witness, just to perform my civic duty as a responsible citizen and all. Who knows what might slip out of my mouth?" She winced and shrugged. "Did you know trial transcripts are a matter of public record? Preserved for posterity. A good thing, since the courtroom is bound to be packed, which means—"

"What do you want?" he snapped.

"It's not what *I* want Mr. Martin, it's what *you* want. *You* very much want Daphne Lavoie to take a plea deal. That avoids the nastiness of a public trial, one with so many messy details spilling out and splashing across the front page of papers."

"And how would one go about making that happen?" he asked in a disgruntled, but very interested tone.

She gave him a thoughtful look. "Well, if they had a more solid case against her, they could easily threaten her with the death penalty if she still insisted on going to trial. In the alternative, she could take a plea, and save her neck. That would have the added benefit of saving the taxpayers the hassle of a trial. The prosecutor would get his win.

You'd be rid of a blackmailer. Everyone is happy! Especially you."

"Then what do you need me for?" he asked in confusion.

"I think it's very much in your best interest to accept Daphne's offer and get her talking, Mr. Martin," Penelope said, giving him a level look. "Today."

The stage was set, so to speak.

Detective Prescott, two police officers, and a very insistent Penelope Banks were hidden in Jameson's executive bathroom. Between the group of them, there were enough witnesses to testify to anything Daphne might have to say.

Jameson's only hope was to get her to reveal enough that she would be foolish to go to trial.

They heard the door open, meaning Daphne had arrived. Penelope couldn't see anything from her vantage point, but she could hear it all perfectly.

"This is to be a one-time offer," Jameson said, using the agreed-upon language. "I don't want to be bothered with this nonsense after today."

Penelope heard Daphne's voice respond. "After today you won't be, so long as I get the amount I requested."

"I need to know what proof it is you have, otherwise there is no deal."

There was a pause as Daphne seemed to mull that over. "Her diary. It's in her handwriting. Including the early days, where she talked about how much money she planned on leeching from you. She was using you, you fool. If I were you, I would be highly embarrassed if it were ever made public."

Penelope could only imagine the look on Jameson's face at hearing that. "She always mentioned how jealous of her you were. Now I see it. She had the talent you didn't. I didn't even have to work that hard to get her into the *Follies*. She just had the star power. Something you're lacking."

Daphne was probably seething at this. Hopefully, it would work. She was a cool customer, so they figured the best way to get her talking was to anger her so she'd rage in a fit of passion, thus revealing everything. A woman like that could quite possibly even gloat about murder.

"A star? Ha!" Daphne spat. "She was nothing more than a cheap harlot. That was her talent, turning men into fools, even that idiot Spanky. She had the audacity to get upset about me coming to you, as though she actually cared for you? As though we couldn't both wet our beaks at the same time? As though I didn't know everything about her?" She laughed. "All so she could stay in her fancy apartment with her fancy clothes and fancy cat. That was almost the best part. Watching her cry over that stupid ball of fur. But not as fun as the look on her face when I told her I could also tell you things about her. That's when she got really mad."

"Is that why you killed her?"

There was a long pause, so long Pen was sure she wouldn't answer.

"I honestly didn't mean to kill her." Daphne uttered this in the same casual tone she would have used if she'd confessed to accidentally selecting the wrong brand of soap at the store. "She just started insulting me, the same way you just did. How I had no talent and was only jealous of her. Looking back, I should have kept a level head. I could have blackmailed her as well. Instead, well...the ice pick was just sitting there. Almost like she had left it out to taunt me.

I was always on drink-making duty during her silly parties." She continued, mimicking Daisy, "'Daphne, you're so good at making drinks, could you *please*?' Well, I showed her what I could do with an ice pick, didn't I?"

Penelope and Detective Prescott turned to look at each other in surprise. She had confessed to the murder of Daisy.

"My God," Jameson whispered.

"Oh stop, don't pretend you cared about her. *Quels imbéciles*," Daphne sneered in French. "You were both idiots, just using each other."

"So are you going to kill me too if I say no? My friend with the police department says you killed this other man as well. What did he have to do with Daisy?"

Again there was a pause. Penelope held her breath, realizing this was the trickier part.

"What is this?" Daphne's voice said in a suspicious tone.

"I just want to know what kind of danger I'm putting myself in with this. My family as well. You don't have to worry about the police. So far I've kept them from taking Daisy's murder seriously. I can keep them from looking into that one as well, I just want to know why you killed him so I can avoid the same fate."

"Pay up and you won't suffer the same fate," Daphne snapped. "*He* was dumb enough to decide he'd rather tell his wife everything instead of pay me. Said she finally deserved to know the truth about him. How the little fool didn't already know was beyond me. The evidence was right there, for heaven's sake." She laughed. "But then, I suppose she wouldn't have been able to understand those letters from his dearly beloved frère. I knew I recognized a French Canadian accent from him."

"So you did kill him?"

"All *you* need to know is that *he's* currently somewhere in the Hudson River with a bullet in him. Do yourself a favor, *JD*, don't suddenly find a conscience, and keep on making sure your friend in the police department sweeps this case under the rug."

Penelope silently inhaled. This was it, an answer to what had happened to Jane's husband. He hadn't left her. He had planned on telling her everything.

And he was most definitely dead.

It would be bittersweet, but at least she'd no longer be left in the dark.

Detective Prescott stared at her, reading it all on her face. When she met his gaze, she smiled, thanking him for helping her get this far.

"Congratulations on solving another case...Penelope."

"Thank you...Richard."

Her smile turned into a grin. She stepped back, allowing the police to do their part.

Penelope had done hers. Her first *major* case as an official lady investigator could finally be closed.

CHAPTER TWENTY-EIGHT

"It seems wrong to celebrate," Jane said, even as she took a sip of champagne on the heels of that.

"We aren't celebrating, we're...heralding in your new future," Penelope improvised, lifting her glass toward her.

They were at the Peacock Club, sitting at a table with Benny while Lulu sang on stage. Jane still had the look of a stunned rabbit at her exotic surroundings, but she was rapidly adjusting to it. The bottle of champagne Penelope had ordered helped.

In the distance, she saw Tommy sitting at a small table by himself. He lazily dragged on a cigarette as he stared at the stage, his mind seemingly lost in thought. Penelope still hadn't taken him up on the offer of a gun, not that she couldn't have purchased one elsewhere, likely via more legal means. At some point, she'd have to take that step if she was going to continue doing this as a career. This case was the second time she'd been in danger for her life.

Considering the intense look on Tommy's face, now was most certainly not the time. She wondered what was going on in the Sweeney family business that had him so focused in thought.

Either way, it certainly wasn't her business and she had no desire to make it so, tonight of all nights.

"Oh hell, celebrate. You've earned it!" Benny said to Jane. That brought Pen's attention back to her table.

Penelope had continued to pay for Jane's room at The Plaza, at least until the media frenzy surrounding the case settled down. She had also given the plucky reporter, Jimmy McDuff his exclusive, spilling details that only an insider would know about.

Of course, Jameson's name couldn't remain a secret for long, despite Daphne taking the plea deal to spare her life and avoid a trial. Penelope was more than happy to dish about his original obstruction in the case of bringing Daisy's killer to justice. JD was most definitely not a happy man these days.

"You have ten thousand dollars to play with now, dove," Benny said. "What are you going to do with it?"

"Why not go to Paris like you always wanted?" Penelope suggested.

Jane gave both of them a bashful look. "I was just thinking about taking a trip up to Ottawa. I just want to see where Frank—*Pierre* came from, learn more about him. I know I should be angry with him but—"

"You don't have to explain yourself to me or anyone else," Penelope said, reaching out to pat her hand. "He was your husband. Your vows were for better or worse, right? You're allowed to mourn him in the way that you see fit. Just make sure you travel up there in first-class style. You deserve that much after what you've been through."

Jane smiled appreciatively.

"And after that? What will you do with yourself?"

"Well, I'm definitely changing my name. I suppose I'll go back to my maiden name."

"What's that?" Benny asked.

"Jane Pugley," she said, frowning into her drink.

Pen and Benny cast quick grimaces at one another but quickly cleared them by the time Jane's attention returned to them.

"On that note, my only request when you end your Canadian adventure is that you *don't* go back to Poughkeepsie," Penelope insisted.

Jane's eyes widened in alarm. "But where can I go?"

"Why not stay here in New York? It can be a wonderful city despite your experience. And now you have new friends—*better* friends," she added, remembering the one so-called friend who had brought her here in the first place.

"But ten thousand dollars, yes it's a lot, but it isn't enough to live on indefinitely. They've taken everything Frank had, not that I'd want to hold onto it knowing how he got it. I can't continue to live at Winchester Court, not after all this. Just the thought of Mrs. Middleberry..."

Penelope could understand the pained expression that came to her face. Her neighbor would secretly revel at the idea of living across from the widow of a murdered outlaw, as much as she would publicly wring her hands over it.

An idea slowly began to form in Penelope's head. She studied Jane. The mild-mannered, timid woman who had come into her office to discover why her husband wasn't dead had gone through enough to change her into something with a bit more fortitude. Perhaps she could build on that?

"How would you like to work with me?"

"With you?"

"Well, I can't promise every case will have a diamond

heist, burglaries, and murder. But there will probably be many missing pets if history is any indication."

Jane laughed. "Oh, I don't know, Miss Banks..."

"Sure you do. And my only requirement is that you for once call me Pen, or if you must maintain your formality, Penelope."

The glow of pleasure coloring her cheeks told Penelope that she just might have a Dr. Watson to her Sherlock Holmes.

EPILOGUE

"Oh, aren't they positively darling!"

Leonard had handed off the basket holding Lady and her three remaining kittens to Chives who was carrying them into the living room, much to Cousin Cordelia's delight.

Pen's cousin instantly rose from the sofa and rushed over to kneel where he set them on the floor.

"Are they ours?"

"It would seem so," Pen said, relieved at her reaction.

Ana had taken the little orange one she favored, being that her husband was agreeable to one cat in their apartment. So little Mila had a permanent home.

Jane had also been smitten with all of them, but finally settled on one orange and white mix, naming her Daffodil. Her new apartment, close to Pen's office was more cozy and humble than the one at Winchester Court, but she had stuck with a Jane Austen theme for her decor. Not *everything* had to change in her life.

Penelope had tried begging some of the other kittens off on her other friends.

Lulu had given her a wry smirk. "There's only one kitty cat I'm interested in caring for and that is me, myself, and I."

Benny had also demurred. "Pen, you should know by now that I am not a *cat* person." She hadn't missed the meaning there.

Detective Prescott had given her a firm no, claiming his schedule didn't allow him to care for a house plant let alone a pet.

So it looked as though Cousin Cordelia and she were parents for the time being to one Lady and her three kittens.

"The mama is named Lady," Pen said, a sad smile coming to her face as she thought of Daisy.

"Oh, how perfect! She looks just like the cat from the pictures in my *Alice in Wonderland* book from when I was a little girl. Lady Dinah, it's perfect! Lady Di for short. I'll have to think of names for the others."

So that was an easy enough problem to solve, though Pen wasn't so sure about an apartment filled with four cats, even as big as it was.

That thought was interrupted by Chives.

"A letter was delivered for you, Miss Banks."

She took the small envelope from him, noting it had no stamp on it so it must have been hand-delivered. "Did you see whom it was from?"

"It was left downstairs with the doorman. I can inquire if you wish?"

"No, don't bother. It isn't important."

Inside was a single sheet of paper. She read what was written.

To Dahlia,

Which answered the question of whom it was from.

Still, Pen was decidedly curious now. What could Spanky possibly have to say to her? She continued:

As you are no doubt aware of by now, my beloved garden has gone to rot. As such, I have decided to sow my seeds in more fertile soil elsewhere, someplace where I can become anonymous once again.

On that subject, I sensed a note of familiarity when I first laid eyes on you. After looking into the Banks family name, I realized where I had seen that ever so slightly impish smile before. You have your mother's eyes as well, though blue instead of the delightfully wicked jade color of hers.

Penelope gasped. Fortunately, Chives was gone and Cousin Cordelia was too preoccupied with her new furry family. She continued reading:

It was in California. I'm not sure how much you know about Miss Juliette Williams...or Sylvine Jade as I knew her back then. She was the lovely daughter of one of the best showmen I'd ever had the pleasure of meeting. Remember what I said about theater being the ultimate fraud?

Your mother was a maestra.

Though it does seem in the end she found happiness in her domestic banality. I'm sure it helped ease the doldrum by marrying a wealthy man.

A shame she had to leave us so soon though. One does wonder how something as trite as the flu was able to take such a dazzling spark upon the universe. Something to consider....

This bit of intelligence is my thank you for helping put Daisy's murderer in prison. You seemed like the type who prefers unwelcome knowledge over blissful ignorance. Forgive me if my intuition was wrong in that regard.

Yours,

Spanky

Penelope stared at the letter, working hard to control her breathing. He'd known her mother?

Sylvine Jade?

All she knew about her mother's past was that her family had been in show business. Everyone had always been vague about the details, much to Pen's disappointment growing up.

But now this.

He had also hinted that she may not have died the way everyone claimed she did, a victim of the Great Flu.

It seemed Penelope had a new and far more important case to look into. It meant talking with her father, something she was loath to do. But this letter couldn't be ignored.

Penelope was taken out of her thoughts by the sound of sneezing behind her. She spun around to find their new maid, Sally continuously sneezing as she entered the living room.

"Cats? *Achoo*! Oh dear, I—*achoo*!—I simply can't—*achoo*!" She waved a hand toward the basket of cats, then quickly left the room, sneezing the entire time.

"Oh no," Penelope muttered.

She turned to give a questioning look to Cousin Cordelia, who already had a firm set to her mouth.

It looked as though they were going to need a new maid.

CONTINUE ON FOR YOUR FREE BOOK!

AUTHOR'S NOTE

As part of the research for this book, I looked into the Prohibition cocktail, the White Lady. The original version created in 1919 called for crème de menthe, triple sec, and lemon juice. It wasn't until 1929 that crème de menthe was replaced with gin and an egg white was added. There are varying accounts as to who originally crafted the drink, with some claiming it was Harry MacElhone and others claiming Harry Craddock

The fun things you learn as an author!

CONTINUE ON FOR YOUR FREE BOOK!

GET YOUR FREE BOOK!

Mischief at The Peacock Club

A bold theft at the infamous Peacock Club. Can Penelope solve it to save her own neck?

1924 New York

Penelope "Pen" Banks has spent the past two years making ends meet by playing cards. It's another Saturday night at The Peacock Club, one of her favorite haunts, and she has her sights set on a big fish, who just happens to be the special guest of the infamous Jack Sweeney.

After inducing Rupert Cartland, into a game of cards, Pen thinks it just might be her lucky night. Unfortunately, before the night ends, Rupert has been robbed—his diamond cuff links, ruby pinky ring, gold watch, and wallet...all gone!

With The Peacock Club's reputation on the line, Mr. Sweeney, aided by the heavy hand of his chief underling Tommy Callahan, is holding everyone captive until the culprit is found.

For the promise of a nice payoff, not to mention escaping the club in one piece, Penelope Banks is willing to put her unique mind to work to find out just who stole the goods.

This is a prequel novella to the *Penelope Banks Murder Mysteries* series, taking place at The Peacock Club before Penelope Banks became a private investigator.

Access your book at the link below:
https://dl.bookfunnel.com/4sv9fir4h3

ALSO BY COLETTE CLARK

PENELOPE BANKS MURDER MYSTERIES

A Murder in Long Island

The Missing White Lady

Pearls, Poison & Park Avenue

Murder in the Gardens

A Murder in Washington Square

The Great Gaston Murder

A Murder After Death

A Murder on 34th Street

Spotting A Case of Murder

The Girls and the Golden Egg

Murder on the Atlantic

A Murder on the Côte D'Azure

A Murder in Blue

A Parisian Murder

LISETTE DARLING GOLDEN AGE MYSTERIES

A Sparkling Case of Murder

A Murder on Sunset Boulevard

A Murder Without Motive

The Cat and the Cadaver

ABOUT THE AUTHOR

Colette Clark lives in New York and has always enjoyed learning more about the history of her amazing city. She decided to combine that curiosity and love of learning with her addiction to reading and watching mysteries. Her first series, **Penelope Banks Murder Mysteries** is the result of those passions. When she's not writing she can be found doing Sudoku puzzles, drawing, eating tacos, visiting museums dedicated to unusual/weird/wacky things, and, of course, reading mysteries by other great authors.

Join my Newsletter to receive news about New Releases and Sales!
https://dashboard.mailerlite.com/forms/148684/72678356487767318/share

Printed in Great Britain
by Amazon